The Paris Express

Born in Dublin in 1969, and now living in Canada, Emma Donoghue writes fiction (novels and short stories, contemporary and historical), as well as drama for screen and stage. Room was shortlisted for the Booker, Commonwealth and Orange Prizes, selling nearly three million copies in forty languages. Donoghue was nominated for an Academy Award for Best Adapted Screenplay for the film adaptation starring Brie Larson. She also co-wrote the screenplay for the film of her novel The Wonder, starring Florence Pugh, and adapted The Pull of the Stars for the stage. For more information, visit www.emmadonoghue.com.

Also by
Emma Donoghue

THE
PARIS
EXPRESS

A novel

Emma
Donoghue

PICADOR

First published 2025 by Summit Books
an imprint of Simon & Schuster
1230 Avenue of the Americas
New York, NY 10020

First published in the UK 2025 by Picador
an imprint of Pan Macmillan
The Smithson, 6 Briset Street, London EC1M 5NR
EU representative: Macmillan Publishers Ireland Limited, 1st Floor,
The Liffey Trust Centre, 117–126 Sheriff Street Upper,
Dublin 1, D01 YC43
Associated companies throughout the world
www.panmacmillan.com

ISBN 978-1-0350-5726-9 HB
ISBN 978-1-0350-5727-6 TPB

Copyright © Emma Donoghue Ltd. 2025

The right of Emma Donoghue to be identified as the
author of this work has been asserted by her in accordance
with the Copyright, Designs and Patents Act 1988.

1 3 5 7 9 8 6 4 2

A CIP catalogue record for this book is available from the British Library.

Printed and bound by CPI Group (UK) Ltd, Croydon, CR0 4YY

Visit www.picador.com to read more about all our books
and to buy them. You will also find features, author interviews and
news of any author events, and you can sign up for e-newsletters
so that you're always first to hear about our new releases.

This book is for my beloved *belle-mère,*
Claude Gillard,
translator and best of readers

The occasional disaster,
What does it matter?
Let's take necessary evils in our stride—
Every great invention costs a few lives!

AUGUSTE-MARSEILLE BARTHÉLEMY,
"STEAM" (1845)

Contents

8:30 a.m.
EMBARK GRANVILLE

There isn't a train I wouldn't take,
No matter where it's going.

EDNA ST. VINCENT MILLAY,
"TRAVEL" (1921)

Half past eight in the morning, on the twenty-second of October, 1895, in Granville, on the Normandy coast. Stocky, plain, and twenty-one, in her collar, tie, and boxy skirt, Mado Pelletier stands across the street from the little railway station holding her lidded metal lunch bucket, watching.

The down train, as they call any service from the capital, deposited Mado here yesterday evening, sooty and bone-jarred. Only now does it occur to her that she could have waited until this morning to leave Paris, disembarked early at Dreux, Surdon, or Flers, bought what she needed, and caught the next express back. All that really matters is that she be on a fast train to Paris by lunchtime on the twenty-second.

She supposes she came all the way to Granville because it's the end of the line. The Company of the West's posters call this wind-raked town the Monaco of the North. In the hours Mado's been here, she hasn't sought out the lighthouse or the casino or any of the so-called sights of this resort, off-season. Except one—she had a hankering to, for once in her life, set eyes on the sea.

It wasn't pretty like everyone said. Wonderfully fierce, in fact—those waves biting into the stones of the beach yesterday evening as the sun went down behind the empty Lady Bathers' hall. Hard to believe in October that invalids flocked here every summer to be wheeled out in bathing machines and half drowned for their health. Mado found a sandy patch and even made an attempt at a castle.

She's always loved being outside, staying out late, spending as little time as possible in the room that has a tang of rot at the back of the Pelletiers' greengrocery in Paris. (It had to hold all four of them when Mado was growing up, but it's just her and her long-faced mother now.) Mado's best memory is of setting off firecrackers in the street one Bastille Day. So this trip to Granville is the kind of thing she'd have enjoyed hugely when she was younger. Not that her parents would ever have been able to spare the money. Like much of the population of the famously wealthy City of Light, even before she was widowed, Madame Pelletier lived by the skin of her teeth.

Her daughter's been planning this trip since she turned twenty-one. Mado spent last night in a room on the unfashionable inland side of the Granville train station, picked at random and paid for with the few coins she hadn't set aside for buying supplies. She blew out the lantern and squeezed her eyes shut for hours at a time, but her mind would never stop buzzing long enough to let her fall asleep.

Up at dawn this Tuesday morning, like a good housewife she did her shopping as soon as the shutters opened. Back in the shabby room, she made her meticulous preparations before leaving in plenty of time to catch the up train to Paris.

So what's preventing Mado from walking into Granville Station now and taking her seat in a Third-Class carriage? What's keeping her feet—still stubby, child-size, in second-hand boots—rooted to the pavement?

Motionless at her side, a small boy with a schoolbag over his shoulders stares at the station entrance as if imitating Mado. She gives him a glare, but his round eyes don't even blink.

Come on, in you go, she tells herself. The strap of her satchel cuts uncomfortably between her breasts.

A fellow glides by on a bicycle, smirking and waggling his eyebrows at her. Mado's been getting this a lot in Granville. That's the price of wearing a tailored jacket with short, oiled-down hair. Even back in Paris, where quite a few young women go about *à l'androgyne*, sneers and jeers have come Mado's way ever since she scraped together the cash to buy this outfit at a flea market last year. Her hair she cuts herself with the razor that was one of the few possessions her father had when he died.

She'll take sneers and jeers over lustful leers any day. Bad enough to have been born female, but she refuses to dress the

3

part. Stone-faced, Mado checks the set of her cravat, then her hat. Her mother's always nagging her to make half an effort to catch a husband when the fact is there's nothing Mado wants less. Even if you got a kind one like her papa, marriage uses you up like a fruit. Mado likes to look at a handsome fellow as much as the next girl, but if the choice is virginity or slavery, she'll take virginity. *Like the Maid of Orléans*, she thinks, straightening her back.

And then: *The Maid of Orléans would be on the blasted train by now. Get moving—unless you mean to miss it?*

Frowning, Maurice Marland looks up at the clock over the station entrance as the Breton guard with the great moustache sent him out to do. Railwaymen are figures of legend to Maurice, and engines are the dragons they command.

The boy lives in the Calvados town of Falaise, more than a hundred kilometres inland. He's taken five rail journeys already in his seven and a half years, but this is the first time he'll be riding alone. Georges had a friend to meet in Granville so couldn't stay to see his little brother settled on the train, but he says Maurice has such a good head on his shoulders that he's ready to travel on his own like a grown man.

The clock shows just past 8:40, the longer hand stabbing the *V* of the *VIII*. That can't be right. Georges told him the Paris Express would be leaving at 8:45, and why would the guard send Maurice outside the station if it's almost time to go?

A trick?

4

Maurice pelts back into the station, ducking under elbows, vaulting a terrier's leash and then a spaniel's, almost tripping over a cane, his face brushing bustles and coats. But this steam engine, which the guard assured him was *a splendid beast and fighting fit*, is showing no signs of motion yet, only hissing through her veils of white and grey.

The Breton takes the chewed pipe out from under his furry handlebar. "What did I tell you about the clock outside, youngster?"

"You said it would surprise me." Maurice's forehead is so furrowed, it aches. "But if the time's gone eight forty already . . . does that mean we're going to be late setting off?"

With a shake of his head, the man points his pipestem at another clock, this one hanging over the platform. It shows 8:36—the minute hand barely nudging past the *VII*. "Time's different inside the station."

Maurice's mouth falls open. When a train takes off, do its crew and passengers somehow stay on this inner time, moving along in an enchanted bubble of five-minutes-behind? That makes no sense, not even for magic. Trains cut through the air so blindingly fast, wouldn't they be, if anything, five minutes *ahead*?

Behind his leathery hand, the guard says: "Stationmaster keeps this clock wound back, doesn't he?"

"Does he?" Maurice's voice a squeak.

"Otherwise half of you would miss the train."

"Half of me?" His eyes bulge. Maurice's left half or his right? Top or bottom half?

"The dawdlers." The guard gestures at the throng.

Maurice puzzles over this, tugging the straps of his schoolbag higher up on his shoulders. So the stationmaster puts back the hands of this clock, the one inside the station, with the result that half the passengers will believe they're boarding on time when in fact they're dawdlers, and the train's been waiting patiently for them. "You mean the Express actually runs five minutes late?"

"Every train in France does."

What a cheat! Railways are pure speed, the most modern thing there is. They're a shortcut to the future, steaming along gleaming metals. So the clocks should all tell true, and the trains should set off on time and leave the dawdlers in the dust.

A gent's voice: "Over here!"

The guard tips out his embers and pockets his pipe. "Coming, monsieur."

Maurice remembers to pull out his brown cardboard ticket, printed with *Third-Class Granville–Paris.* "You haven't clipped this yet."

He only nods. "Don't lose that—you'll need to show it when you get down at Dreux. And don't let anyone take anything off you."

What might they try to take—Maurice's lunch wrapped in waxed paper? His milk bottle stoppered with a clean rag?

The guard grabs a T-shaped handle on the train above him and pulls open a brown door, beckoning.

Maurice hurries over, ready to climb the iron steps. But

the man seizes the back of his collar and the belt that keeps up Georges's hand-me-down trousers and hoists Maurice into the carriage like a dog. "Dreux—remember."

Affronted, straightening his seams, Maurice nods over the half-lowered pane in the door. How could he forget the name of the station east of Falaise, the name Georges has drilled into him, the place where Papa has business this week, where Papa will be waiting for Maurice in the cart outside the station at 2:20 this afternoon?

He glances over his shoulder but can't spot anywhere to sit. He's embarrassed for all these strangers to see him harbouring designs on their benches; they probably think he's a *dawdler*. So for now Maurice stays at the door as if he prefers standing, eyes fixed on the mud-brown wall covered with words and pictures—*Louriste Razors, Valda Pastilles, The Divine Sarah, Smoke Gauloises, Irisine Beauty Powder, Liebig Meat Extract, St. Raphael Quinine, Rochet Bicycles, Colle-Bloc Glues Everything*—as if he's enclosed in a book, a sturdy volume with the power to carry these people all the way to Paris.

On the platform below, the bookstall's yellow awning says *Hachette: Banish Monotony and Ennui*. The word *banish* makes Maurice think of villains sent abroad and never allowed to return to France. Georges says if Maurice listens to his elders and reads every spare minute he gets, one day he'll know all the words there are and could even be a schoolteacher. Before his brother hurried out of Granville Station this morning, he bought Maurice a brand-new story about an Englishman circumnavigating the globe in eighty days, which sounds impossible, but Maurice doesn't think the book would be called *Around the World in Eighty Days* if the hero failed.

His right hand turns over the hoard of shells in his pocket. These few days in Granville were his first encounter with the sea. The rock pools! The wide, blustery beach where big boys were flicking stones at the waves and each other in a game that seemed to get more hilarious the closer they came to shedding blood.

Papa's from the Normandy town of Caen, and Maman's always lived in nearby Falaise; they've buried a baby in each town, which is what she calls *a root that never breaks*. But it strikes Maurice that when he's grown to be a man, he could choose to move away and settle on the coast, where he could smell this salt breeze every day. Is that what a holiday is, a glimpse of another, larger life?

An exotic-looking woman glides along the platform—no, it's a man in a skirt, a limp skirt all the way down to his sandals; Maurice can see the fellow's bare brown toes. An extraordinary tank on the man's back wobbles high above his brimless cap, with . . . could that be steam leaking out of the top? The appliance has its own long wooden leg behind. Is the little man half machine?

A gent in a top hat with a valise puts his hand up, and the foreigner produces a tiny handleless cup and fills it with brown liquid from a tap on his chest. *He's a human coffeepot!* The gent pays and tries to walk away with his drink, but he's brought up short by the thinnest of chains attaching the cup to the tank; that makes Maurice grin. Top Hat has to knock back the drink in one go before he hurries off, leaving the wet cup dangling.

Here's the guard again, snatching two cases off a cart as if they weigh no more than pillows ...

Jean Le Goff settles passengers in carriages with the tolerant air of one who has stepped away from important business to do them a favour; that makes them more inclined to offer him a *pourboire*. Not yet thirty, he keeps the points of his great handlebar waxed, hoping the combination of peaked cap, pipe, and moustache will add a few years. (Jean would quite fancy a goatee but the Company of the West frowns on beards.) Le Goff—or "Ar Goff," the way they say it in Brittany—means "blacksmith," and the men in Jean's family are squarely built; he keeps his shoulders set in a soldierly fashion. He did register with the military at twenty, as required by law, but he's never been called up, as they don't need so many soldiers in peacetime. At any rate, it does no harm to give the impression of having served, since every second railwayman is a veteran. Jean lets passengers thank him for his patriotism as they dig deeper in their pockets.

He prefers to keep Rear First vacant at the start of the day in case someone awfully rich needs to board later. So he tries to induce First-Class passengers to bunch up in the front carriage of their two in the middle of the train rather than spread out over both. They're mostly hard-to-please Parisians, but he supposes their reluctance to share is understandable;

the whole point of paying top rates is to stretch out in something like a private sitting room—except, of course, that it's rattling through the countryside on wheels.

Jean opens the green door of Front First and ushers in an older gent with a wooden arm and a family of three complete with a yappy cocker spaniel. He seats them on the plump red velvet banquettes and sucks up mightily—stows their hatboxes, bags, muffs, shawls, and canes in the nets overhead, arranges travel rugs over laps as if it were deepest January instead of October, tucks hats by their brims under the taut strings that run along the ceiling for storage ... shall he pull back the lace-edged curtains and put the blind up? Half up—just so; he adjusts it tenderly by its tassel. Turn up the lamps for reading? No need, no weak eyes among this party. Very good, and yes, the oil does smoke rather.

The spaniel spins and yips. "Animals are really supposed to be kept in their baskets in one of the baggage vans," Jean mentions.

"Oh, but Ouah-Ouah would be lonely. He'd whine." The girl's so wan, she's almost greenish.

"He promises to be good," the mother says.

Must be nearly tip time, especially if Jean's going to turn a blind eye to the dog. He drops a hint about the radiator's being freshly filled with boiling water.

"Oh, a footwarmer for our daughter too, please."

Merde! Tell First Class what you've already done for their comfort, and you prompt them to ask for more.

"I wouldn't bother, *ma chère*," the husband tells the wife, "they're always stone-cold after an hour."

A show of brains can shake the money tree, so Jean puts in, "Ah, but we use acetate of soda now, which holds on to the heat longer."

The gent looks impressed.

Jean jumps down to the platform to grab the girl a footwarmer—but he's distracted by a dark young lady tugging at the door of Rear First. "Locked, I'm sorry to say, mademoiselle."

"Could you open it, please?"

She hasn't reached for her purse, and judging from her plain blue outfit, she's not a lavish tipper, so Jean lies: "Very likely that one's being taken off before Paris."

She sighs, switching her cumbersome case—some kind of sewing machine?—from one hand to the other. A *femme de couleur*, Jean would guess—mixed ancestry—and she'd be quite pretty if she took a little trouble.

He hands her up the steps into Front First, where the one-armed gent is already occupying the tiny mahogany table with a notebook and pen. The family man's immersed in a copy of this morning's *Granvillais*, its ink still damp. The four make room for the intruder civilly. But the footwarmer Jean meant to get for this young girl! There's never enough time at stops, and more than once he's forgotten a passenger's request and missed his chance to earn a tip. "Just one more minute, mademoiselle."

He lopes along the platform to the bubbling cistern. He hooks one of the oval metal footwarmers, grips it with a rag, and canters back to Front First to get . . . fifty centimes in copper from the father. Could be worse. That'll buy bread and cheese and coffee or a condom, depending on what he's in the mood for at the end of his shift in Paris.

Jean pulls out the heavy disc of his watch: No more time. At Christmas all crewmen receive up to a full month's pay for *good work*, which boils down to keeping their train on schedule. He rushes down the train to position himself in Rear Baggage, where the junior guard always rides as if ready for any danger from behind. (Brigands galloping down the track?) Or in case the convoy wrenched apart in the middle, Jean supposes, so the second half wouldn't be left unmanned. Or, more realistically, so that if they were rammed from the back by a train with a drunk or dozing driver, it would be Rear Baggage that got staved in; injured passengers or bereaved families might sue, but crewmen (like soldiers) accepted the risks that came with the job.

Well, these unlikely hypotheticals don't weigh heavy on Jean. At the start of every journey, Rear Baggage is an empty box, his haven from all the demands to come. Soon he'll have his first long smoke lounging in his chair with his feet up on the desk he uses only for that purpose.

At the front of the train, driver Guillaume Pellerin's taken up his position on the iron footplate. A thick drawbar links his engine to the tender that holds her coal bunker and water tank. His stoker, Victor Garnier, stands at his left in the same red scarf to the chin and cap over his ears as Guillaume. There's no cab to sit in, not so much as a stool to rest their arses; the Company prefers its rollers on their toes throughout the journey. The Express has a crew of four, including the guards, but only the driver and stoker count as *rollers*—royals among railwaymen.

Victor Garnier's greying bush of a moustache masks his mouth, but Guillaume can always tell if his mate's in good humour, which he is this morning.

Three Third-Class carriages, two Firsts, two Seconds, one baggage van at the back and another at the front, and a post van behind the tender, which means almost a dozen vehicles for Engine 721 to pull; Guillaume's known this great hog to haul seventeen, though he'd never agree to more than twenty. Her train is put together at Granville every second night by a coupler who ducks beneath undercarriages, deft with his shunting pole. (Guillaume's seen a slow mover get his leg carved right off at the knee.) The Granville yardmen have been up half the night swabbing because the least speck can clog a valve but also for pride in the machine. They've greased her, topped up her oil and sand, and used a high dumper to load her tender with the best black-brown coal. Hours ago they raked out her firebox and threw in a paraffin stick to light her up, so she'll have time to warm up. With a hydraulic crane, they've filled the U-shaped water jacket around her bunker with a tankful pumped out of the Boscq. (Victor's very fierce about getting only pure river water; any silt of clay or salt could bung up her pipes.)

Guillaume and his stoker have been here since half past six this morning. He's tried the regulator, reverser, air brake, hand brake, and steam whistle to make sure each wheel and handle moves as it should. Down by his feet, the drain cocks and the sanding gear are in good order. He doesn't need to ask whether Victor's checked his boiler controls on the left— the pressure gauge, safety valve, water-level glass, injector wheel, and dampers.

They're both family men. Guillaume spends every second evening with his Françoise and their little boy in their lodgings just off the tracks, a kilometre before Montparnasse Station in Paris, where the rooms shake every time a train goes by. And Victor lives with his Joséphine by Montparnasse Cemetery, ten minutes' walk from Guillaume's. The mates never see each other in the city, as their wives don't get on, but they spend ten days out of every eleven elbow to elbow on the footplate of Engine 721 and every second night in the same boardinghouse in Granville. Even their work clothes have merged over the years; they grab smock shirts, soft jackets, denim trousers, and caps from the one parcel the laundrywoman sends back.

Guillaume wears boots, but Victor prefers clogs so he can stamp out a flaming cinder without setting his soles on fire. He cracks four eggs into a puddle of butter on his shovel to test the fire's heat.

How they crackle! Guillaume's stomach is empty, harsh

with a morning shot of black coffee and red wine. He breaks a roll and leans over the glowing red metal.

"Wait!" Victor says.

Guillaume laughs under his breath.

"One more minute," Victor insists, holding Guillaume's sleeve.

"But you always overdo the eggs."

"Half a minute, then."

Guillaume bumps him aside, dips his bread. The two fight to mop up the slithering gold. *Merde, that's good.* They burp and wipe their mouths. Victor scrubs at his moustache with a handkerchief that's not yet grimy. Some of the men call him Walrus; only Guillaume knows that his stoker grew it from the age of twelve to hide the puckered scar from a cleft lip.

Nothing's hurting Guillaume yet, and the day promises fair weather. "What kind of trip are we going to have, mate?" His customary question.

"Fast but smooth," Victor assures him.

Guillaume cracks his tight knuckles one by one. "Smooth but fast."

Blonska's bones are sixty years old and feel more like a hundred. She stirs on the platform where she curled up last night between a pillar and a barrel, neither of which kept the Granville wind at bay. The sea breeze, the locals call it, as if it's some soft zephyr rather than a knife of air. Her eyes are cemented shut; she rubs the crumbs away. She tries to sit up.

May have overdone it this time, kipping on flagstones. But what else was Blonska supposed to do when she found the platform had no benches? This morning she might not be able to get to her feet in time to board the Express before it blasts away. If she has to be carted off to hospital—if this seaside town even has one—it'll mean further worry and expense for the Parisian ladies who sent her here for a fortnight to restore her health. (Blonska's eyes have been red and blurred, her twisted spine more trouble than usual.)

This modern notion of needing to go away on holiday for one's health is an invention of the railway companies, in her view, but it would have seemed churlish to refuse her patrons outright. Still, she didn't feel obliged to spend *all* their money on her own trivial comfort, and a week seemed more than long enough for a rest. So last Tuesday she came down in Third Class instead of First, as it would have offended her intelligence to waste twenty-seven francs on a seat just to be in a prettier carriage. She took one look at Granville's Hôtel des Bains—facing the shore, all froufrou gingerbread and ruched curtains—and turned away towards the steps clambering up the cliff. She found a much cheaper room in an alley where the wind whipped across the high town, rented out by the wife of a fisherman who was off in Newfoundland after cod for half the year. She also saved the money her patrons had given her for meals, instead munching on nuts and apples as she looked out at the island of Jersey and sucked in the free salt air.

Hard to catch her breath on this busy platform, though, after the cold night on the ground. Blonska's dressed in her patrons' gauzy hand-me-downs; she has no objection to fine wrappings if they're free, even if they look queer on an old spinster bent over like a question mark. Back in Russia, before any journey, you sat down on your baggage for a quiet moment to gather your forces. But Blonska has brought only a satchel, to save the effort of toting a suitcase, and it's time to stop stalling and get up. When she tips back her head, she realises that the iron and glass roof of the station needs to be this high to make room for the steam and smoke; a low ceiling would trap passengers and crew in a blinding fog.

All of a sudden, a whistle makes her jump, and her back spasms—the moustachioed guard's giving the first warning of departure. She scrapes herself off the flagstones and lurches to her knees, then to her numb feet. Only her orthopaedic corset holds her up. This was a surprisingly useful present, moulded to her exact misshape, so she hasn't passed it on to someone needier.

Sometimes Blonska accepts lavish gifts to soothe the givers' unease; it's only in the privacy of her mind that she mutters, *Go to hell with your bonbons and your fortifying wines.* It's a fact that society would be rather less terrible if the bonbons, wines, and francs were more evenly distributed, so Blonska plays her part by letting the guilty philanthropic ladies of Paris use her as a faceted lemon-squeezer on which to press their wealth.

Third Class is always placed at the front of the train so as to catch the brunt of the coal dust and of course so that in the event of a head-on collision, those in the cheap seats will do their duty by getting crushed before their betters. The middle of the three brown doors is hanging open just a few steps away. Blonska might move with the frail, bobbing glide of a seahorse, but she's a tough old boot. She heaves her satchel upward and pushes it onto the splintering floor of the carriage, then gets one worn sole on the metal step, claws at the handrail, and drags herself up and in.

She scans the pairs of long wooden benches facing each other. She inches through the narrow gap down the middle of the carriage. The air is thick with tobacco, garlic, whiskey, linseed oil, and wet straw. Ah, a gap; Blonska drops into it. She leans her shoulder blades against the narrow back bar. Catching her breath, she peers past somebody's hat at the steamed-up window. She'll have a view north this time, all the way home to Paris. She'll enjoy the scenery, even if the lush green fields of lower Normandy aren't a patch on the Great Steppes.

She takes her knitting out of her satchel because she can knit by feel. She'd love to read on the journey—she's halfway through Chekhov's latest stories—but she must keep resting her eyes or she'll be no use to Monsieur Claretie this week. Blonska has a part-time job looking after his library at the Comédie-Française and takes pride in this slim connection to the oldest theatre company in existence. She's put in order the books and papers of other men of letters as well (less for money than out of her itch for tidiness)—the tireless reformer Clemenceau, for instance, who calls her *stubborn old Blonska*. She was baptised Elise, but these fellows use only her surname, almost as if she's one of them.

A fisherwoman opposite has a startlingly intricate strip of Bayeux lace over her muscular shoulders. She's holding a great basket of oysters that pokes Blonska's knees and is already causing complaints from a man in a bowler hat.

"Fresh out of the sea," the oysterwoman tells him without turning her head, "and the sea's all you can smell, so don't dare say otherwise."

"Well, I just hope they don't start stinking by Paris."

"Cold day in October? No fear of that."

"Can one of you pull down the blind to keep the sun off them?" he grumbles.

"Oi!" Several voices are raised in protest at the idea. Blonska nods; she's still chilled to the bone and would miss the bit of sunshine.

The bowler-hat man sucks on his pipe. "Well, can you move the basket so we've got some elbow room?"

"Move it where?" the fisherwoman wants to know.

"Put it on the floor."

"Can't have no dirt or ash getting on my oysters."

"Such prices you lot charge," the bowler hat says, "Granvillais can't afford a taste of our own shellfish anymore."

The oysterwoman pulls a faux-sympathetic face. "Have to sell high, don't I, to cover the ticket to Paris and back?"

"Or you could save yourself the trouble of going—stay home and sell them cheaper. It's not as if it takes long to pull a few oysters off the rocks."

"Risking my life in those storms, and the highest tides in Europe? If you think it's that easy, go pull your own!"

Blonska's seen fistfights break out in Third before, but this argument has a lazy tone to it; the two locals are just passing time.

"Well." The oysterwoman sighs. "Poor people's bread always burns."

Nobody's inclined to disagree with that old saw.

The man with the bowler hat folds his coat into a lumpy cushion to sit on. Blonska would do the same with her shawl if she didn't need it to keep the chill off her chest.

"They make it as uncomfortable as they possibly can, don't they?" he throws her way.

She smiles. "On purpose, monsieur—you think?"

"The Company's trying to force anyone with the cash to fork out for Second. See these tiny holes drilled in the floor to make draughts?"

Sceptical, Blonska bends over—but the man's right, there are pinpricks at regular intervals.

On the whole, she's relieved to have her holiday behind her and to be heading back with more than two hundred francs stuffed in her corset. (She can't imagine any robber bold enough to rifle through her damp wrappings.) Blonska will have the satisfaction of handing over the cash to the next person she meets who needs it for rent, shoes, coal and candles, bread and milk. Having somehow made it to the advanced age of sixty despite all her ailments, she likes to see how long she can sit on a winter day without lighting a fire; scrimping gives her a little shiver of triumph. That's conceited in its own way, Blonska knows; everyone has his or her vanity, and doing without happens to be hers.

Perhaps this will be her last long trip. Life's too short to make a habit of travelling arduously to faraway places and doing nothing there in hopes of bolstering your powers so you can do useful things again for a little longer. Why not just keep trying to be useful until the whistle blows?

It's best to be prepared. Long ago Blonska entrusted a hundred francs to her employer Monsieur Claretie to be used to bury her decently. Varvara Nikitine, whom Blonska lived with for two years, has left space for her friend in her own plot in Montparnasse Cemetery. (Varvara was touring Ireland to study poverty when she caught pleurisy and died of it.) You can't cheat the hourglass; the sand will run out whether you're watching it or not. *Forward over the graves*, as Goethe wrote after the death of his last child.

Senior guard Léon Mariette checks to ensure he has all his necessary kit: timetable, rule book, pencil, log (squared paper covered in black cloth and closed with an elastic band), medical kit, pocket torch, whistle, carriage keys, signal flags in red, green, and white. He relishes the weight of responsibility, unlike young Jean Le Goff, who gets by with a penknife, a flashy waistcoat and tie, and a ridiculous moustache.

Léon has followed the departure protocols; he's walked the length of the platform with a station guard (a former stoker deafened by the work). They've scanned every coupling and sprung buffer to make sure they're sound and oiled with a pair of side chains hooked on as a backup but loosely enough to give some play where the train will need to curve with her tracks. Sometimes those turnbuckle screws work loose, or the chains crack, or dishonest railwaymen nick bits and sell them for scrap. In Léon's experience, the Company of the West is infested with thieves, shirkers, and time-wasters.

Crews can be just as stupid as civilians; they cut corners and rebel against the rules. Few seem to grasp that accidents don't happen by accident. Léon thinks of the railways as a hard school in which making the least slip can kill an innocent person. A stage upon which character is revealed in a merciless light . . . but unlike at the theatre, on the railways, justice is not done.

Now he's making sure that every door is shut and every handle horizontal. He wishes he could grab the last few stragglers like stray chickens and toss them into their hutches. He's already heard Le Goff's first whistle—pert, almost cocky—so he hurries all the way to the train's nose to check that the kerosene headlamp is burning well above the Company plaque that says *West*. The smokebox is like a great clock with no hands, and the steel blade (for snow or other obstructions) is gleaming below.

Moving at a trot, Léon doubles back to Front Baggage, his base for the journey, and climbs in just in time to hear Le Goff's final warning whistle. He mounts the short ladder to perch in the senior guard's birdcage, a lantern-shaped lookout on the roof. He glances down at the platform and sees a young woman with a lidded tin lunch bucket dash out of nowhere and up the steps of Rear Third.

"Too late," Léon roars at her. More than a few fools have brought death on themselves by leaping on or off at the last moment.

She has the cheek to ignore him, this peculiar person, upright as a toy soldier in a straight skirt, a collar and tie, brilliantined hair cut to just below the ears, a worn slouch hat. Paris fashion—Léon will never understand it. But she's wrestled the carriage door open and leapt in, and here comes the dignified note of the steam whistle, Guillaume Pellerin formally asking permission for departure. Only once the Granville guard clangs his handbell does Léon lift his own whistle from his chest to give the sharp all-clear. Some gripe that you could shave a minute off the whole ritual by cutting out this exchange of sounds, but as Léon always says, *Better prepare and prevent than repair and repent.*

Sometimes ignorant civilians or even fellow railwaymen, who should know better, address Senior Guard Mariette as if he's a mere baggageman, a creature of labels and ledgers, when the fact is, the lives of more than a hundred persons are in his experienced hands. Up in his birdcage, he has the most comprehensive view of train and track, and an alarm bell hangs to his right in the event of his spotting danger ahead or behind.

Also, he plays an unseen but not unimportant role in actually driving the train. Every time Pellerin moves the train out, Léon fingers the leather binding of his hand brake and leans a little on the crank, which turns a screw under the floor and presses the iron teeth softly against the wheels to smoothen the gathering movement. Without that, the links of the train can jerk, which Léon feels just like the ache in his hips at the end of each day. (He turned forty-one this year.) He wishes passengers would understand that *rolling stock* is called that because it rolls; it's in the nature of its pieces to lag a little behind or leap ahead or nudge each other. Do these people expect to glide halfway across France in a day as smoothly as angels on a cloud? And it's Senior Guard Mariette, the public face of the Company, who's obliged to present himself on the platform at every halt station, patient and accountable. Those who complain of being *yanked about*, let them take it up with the Maker, who neglected to polish the Earth like a billiard ball.

Léon skews around to check himself in the Front Baggage van's small mirror. His muttonchop whiskers are sharply trimmed; his stiff, black, flat-topped kepi reminds him of the red one from his army days. (As it was peacetime, he was mostly assigned to protect railway lines in West Africa— keeping order as civilisation advanced across the continent one kilometre at a time.) His buttoned-on shirt collar is fresh this morning and his grey coat is fastened all the way down his thighs over its matching jacket. This makes it rather hard for Léon to bend at the waist, but what's the point of having standards if they're to be let slip?

The Paris Express is properly underway now, so he releases

the hand brake and allows himself a moment's ease, watching the last shuttered houses of Granville flick by.

——————

Moving at last!

She is how the crew refer to the train, out of fondness but also to mark the distinction between her and them. Technically, she is Engine 721, a six-wheeled locomotive constructed for the Company of the West eighteen years ago. But in another sense, she is this whole train, since without the coal and water in the tender coupled on behind her, she couldn't huff and puff and move her wheels, and without the long, thick chain of carriages assembled afresh every night, she'd have no reason to move.

From the tip of Normandy, she cuts due east, like a spoon taking the top off the lightly boiled egg of France. Every passenger, whether paying nine francs to squeeze into one of her Third-Class carriages, eighteen for Second, or twenty-seven for First, will be treated to the luxury of speed. Today's trip of three hundred and twenty-six kilometres should be interrupted by only four brief stops. Barring acts of God, caprices of Nature, mishaps, or human failings, she should pull into Paris-Montparnasse in seven hours and ten minutes, at 3:55 p.m.

Why should you take an interest in this particular railway journey? France has one of the densest meshes of tracks on earth. The iron vine writhes across the plains, bores through the mountains, leaps the rivers. Every hour of the day, trains shatter the quiet, char the air, and scare the wildlife. So why care about this one express from Granville on the morning of the twenty-second of October, 1895?

Not because she's bound for Paris. Most trains go to or from that knot at the top of the net, the spider at the heart of the web. It's prohibitively expensive to ship goods anywhere other than the capital, but that's where the majority of customers live anyway. For half a century, the six companies have extended their routes like spokes radiating from the great hub of Paris.

No: What's remarkable about this train is that she's heading straight for disaster.

Every journey must come to an end, after all. As a Scottish saying has it: Hours are time's arrows, and one of them is fletched with death.

8:45 a.m.
DEPART GRANVILLE

And here is a mill and there is a river;
Each a glimpse and gone forever!

ROBERT LOUIS STEVENSON,
"FROM A RAILWAY CARRIAGE" (1885)

The first of the two Second-Class carriages at the rear of the train has just one occupant, Henry Tanner. The American painter leans back against the partition's padded section, which is covered in only slightly worn blue corduroy. Granville Station reminded Henry of Monet's dozen canvases of Paris's Gare Saint-Lazare—like landscapes but indoors, with smoke and steam for clouds, diffusing the light that beams through the glass roof. It strikes him that it's not easy to portray the passing of time in a picture. The old masters relied on symbolism (sundials, hourglasses, snuffed candles, and skulls) or personification—old Father Time in his silvery beard. But what Monet managed to catch in each of his train canvases was a sense of the fleeting. Henry wishes he could paint only half so well.

He sits with his knees wide, trying to relax. He's been roughing it out west in Brittany, where you can scrape by on fifty francs a month if you lodge on a farm. After the summer's economies, Henry could possibly afford to treat himself to a ride in First Class, but here he is in Second, because—though he knows it's silly—he'd find First too much of a strain on the nerves.

Not that he would have reason to be nervous—French railways don't have any rule about who's allowed sit where. If Henry were riding a train south from New York, say, then when he reached Washington, DC, he'd be forced to change to the small Coloured car that reeks of the conductors' urine. His jaw tightens at the memory. No, France has a much better claim to being the land of *liberté, égalité*, and all that.

But if Henry were to travel in First from Granville today . . . well, even if none of his fellow passengers insinuated that the gentleman might have stepped through the green door by mistake, or even if they failed to read him as a *noir*, he'd be tense all the way to Paris. So why borrow trouble? Besides, this blue upholstery is quite comfortable, really. Henry's used to much worse; the studio he shares with a pal from the American Art Association is in a ramshackle building in Montparnasse, loud with the tubercular hacking of artists and models.

He stares out the window to distract himself from the torment of self-consciousness. Small fields and winding lanes sunken between high hedgerows tangled with brush and nettles. Telegraph poles along the track, birds on the wires like notes in a musical score. The train dips down into a cutting, then climbs up on an embankment. Strips of cultivated land radiate from a village. A small, walled-off cemetery, the ghetto of the dead, followed by stubble; Henry supposes late October must be a respite between wheat harvest and sowing?

A knot of peasants by the track, faces turned towards the passing Express. Do they come just to watch these great machines zip by? The railway can't be a novelty anymore, surely. Maybe it is just an excuse to gather and chat.

Half-timbered houses, rather Anglo-Saxon to American eyes, since the northwest is the part of France that the English held longest. There's one with what Henry recognises as a hawthorn bush planted by the door—to ward off lightning, a farmer told him. Steep roofs in pinkish flat tile, grey slate. Henry much prefers the old thatch to red corrugated iron. He's going by so fast, it's hard to catch all the architectural details. That's the paradox of trains, he supposes; they show you what you'd never have seen otherwise, but only for a tantalising second.

He spent half his youth staring till his eyes hurt. When each of those Philadelphia art teachers in turn turned down the *mulatto boy*, Henry made do; he'd stand for hours in a free gallery studying a landscape, then scurry home to reproduce it from memory. But at last Mr. Eakins took him on and opened the whole world to him. Eakins had his students paint straight colour onto primed canvas without the safety net of a preparatory sketch. He told them, *There are no lines in Nature.*

The motion of the train is making Henry a little queasy. He should have had more of a breakfast in Granville. His first winter in Paris, he couldn't adjust to starting the day French-style with just coffee and a roll instead of beefsteak and griddle cakes. In the evenings, he had a similar problem—waiters threw him out of cafés for failing to order wine like a Frenchman. Eventually he taught himself to get through a small glass in sips; when in Rome and all that.

Henry finds he's watching out for anything picturesque. A huge pear tree, self-seeded, splits the ruin of a cottage. A road mender working with bucket and spade on a pale, dust-haloed track as straight as the railway line with a stand of plane trees along each side. Two children in a cart—that could be an appealing subject . . . except that they're being pulled by a tired dog. (The French have no sentimentality about animals, but such a scene would appal a British or American picture-buyer.)

A man with a massive basket on his back, saucepans dangling. Tantalising; if the tiny figure were closer, Henry could get out his little camera and capture a quick study for later. (Call it *Normandy Pedlar? Tinker Crossing Field?*)

Art is a profession of vagabonds, Reverend Tanner intones in his son's head.

To settle his ragged breathing, Henry thinks about his painting. Not one of the small seascapes parcelled up with his trunk in the baggage van but the large, unfinished *Daniel*, facing the wall in his studio in Paris. He needs to capture that moment when, thrown into the stinking pit, the prophet didn't rail or fight the lions but sat down and prayed. Henry has a rectangle of honeyed evening light sliding into the prison from a high window, and he's setting cool blues against the lions' yellow fur. He wants to show time stop as the prophet's voice gentles the beasts. (So many visits Henry's made to the Jardin des Plantes to sketch the caged lions in their various discontented poses.) *Please, Lord, teach me to paint it right.*

The heroes of the Old Testament endured such terrors stoically; why does Henry tremble at the prospect of a fellow passenger giving him a curious look or the hugely moustachioed guard asking to see his Second-Class ticket? *You are Henry Ossawa Tanner*, he scolds himself, *and you have every right to be on this train.*

Every minute or so, Victor Garnier turns to squint into the bunker, with its broad chute tilted down towards him, and smashes open a few big lumps with the back of his shovel. If the coal's very dusty, he sprinkles it with water from a bucket at his feet. He thrusts his shovel into the mass to fill it with ten kilos' worth; hoists and pivots and heaves it across the footplate without dropping a crumb, missing his mate by a hair, all while hauling open the firebox door with his left clog. A great wash of light and heat blasts in the rollers' faces from the molten flow, the colour of fresh blood. Victor shoves the coal down the ramp, deep into the furnace's flaming maw, rakes the coals, then slams the door with his right foot.

Next he grasps the rail with his right hand and leans way out to the left of the train to check that the rails ahead are clear. There are two small portholes in the iron backhead in front of him, one on each side of the boiler, but Victor can never make out much through the filthy glass. Overhead, a half metre of roof to keep the worst of the weather off. The stoker wears his goggles to shield his eyes from smuts because he's known tough fellows too careless to wear them who've ended up blinded. No gloves, though, not this side of Christmas; Victor's grip is better without. Wind buffets the hair escaping from his cap; when he opens his mouth to cough, the air cuts right through his red muffler and makes his teeth ache.

Two clogs planted back on the thrumming footplate, he finds his balance again. He eyes the smoke streaming from the chimney overhead; not too much, and light grey rather than black, that's good. When Engine 721's in motion, the roaring is so loud that he and Guillaume Pellerin can't exchange a word. Not that they need to after all these years.

One man in two bodies, that's how Victor thinks of himself and his driver. He's the younger fellow's right-hand man, though always standing on Guillaume's left. (An old joke.) Outsiders assume Victor's the brainless one. Feed the hog and slake her thirst—couldn't a half-wit with a shovel do that much? The truth is, there's nothing simple about supplying steam, just the right amount of it at just the right moment. Speed is the special task laid on Guillaume, and thrift is on

Victor, but both the rollers work to save the Company money while keeping on schedule.

What bothers Victor—what the pencil pushers can't seem to grasp—is that the two goals are incompatible. Getting to Paris at exactly 3:55 today is possible only if the crew of four and every station porter and guard along the way does his job exactly right. It's almost always passengers, with their last-minute requests and confusions, who cause delay. In order not to inconvenience these same passengers, any time lost must be made up somehow, which means the Company allows driver and stoker to put on speed—but only up to a point, for safety's sake.

And quite apart from increasing the risk of accidents, speed eats too much coal, oil, and grease. The Company's so desperate that every month that a skilled pair of rollers saves on these supplies, they are rewarded with a bonus of up to forty percent. Forty! That's the difference between Joséphine's sigh and her smile, the gap between getting by and feeling rich.

At least he and Guillaume are partners in this demanding enterprise, day after day. Not equals, of course; a great hog can have only one master, and Pellerin is among the very best. He's climbed the ladder fast, not only making driver by thirty-five but always assigned express trains, the pedigreed racers of the fleet. Twice he's been cited for outstanding acts of vigilance, which Victor happens to know from the *Bulletin*; his mate would never mention it. Always careful and scrupulous—is it any wonder Guillaume's chocolate-brown eyes have a slightly hunted look?

He often says he couldn't move their engine a metre without Victor. On winter days, both of them suffer frozen backs and scalded chests at the same time, their hands and forearms perpetually branded with scars and burns.

Pastures and woods blur by now. Out of the corner of his eye, Victor sees Guillaume glance his way. He grins and nods back with the usual thumbs-up.

In the Middle Third carriage, John Synge is labouring away with a pencil, making notes.

Balancing on the shaking boards between the benches like a circus equestrian, a coffee seller—North African, John would guess—has a towering tank strapped tightly to his back. The young Dubliner has never seen such an apparatus; he sketches it, inch-high.

The coffee seller opens a tap on his chest now and pours the black stuff deftly through a filter made of woven leaves into a small horn cup on a chain. He takes a sip of his own brew and sighs. Sincerely relishing the coffee, John wonders, or advertising to the carriage? Or both?

The passenger to John's left turns the page of yesterday's *Little Parisian*, chuckling to himself. A mongrel terrier is tucked behind his heels, and a hat is upturned on his lap.

John tilts over just enough to make out the worn letters inked inside the man's hatband: DOIS. He likes the name and copies it down. John's writing all the time these days, though not a sentence worth reading yet. He's just a collector, letting vivid impressions of the world, whatever comes his way, soak into him.

He enjoys all forms of movement—cycle rides, hikes on which he can strike up brief conversations with tramps and labourers—but perhaps most of all, train journeys. The scenes briefly framed in the window form a continuous, unpredictable drama of happenstance. And inside the carriage, too, it's all go, especially when a train's chockablock. The main reason John travels in Third Class is to stretch the meagre remittances Mama sends from their Dublin suburb, but it also lets him study characters, the more colourful the better.

The girl in the extravagantly feathered hat smoking opposite him, for instance. Her small, stern features could come from anywhere between Bombay and Manila. By her clothes she announces herself as a demimondaine, the kind Mama would denounce as *a denizen of Gomorrah*. John has shaken off all those old pieties; he'd never resort to hiring one of these women, but they wake in him a private, tender sympathy.

The smoker's hat bears a taxidermied nestful of slightly crumpled black and orange orioles. Her flame-coloured dress is billowing over John's knees, and . . . God Almighty, is that a live monkey on her shoulder grinning out from her huge chignon, the morning sun haloing it with red-gold?

Next his eyes are drawn to the passenger beside the plumed girl, a woman with a cone-shaped head, her baby on her lap with its skull tightly bandaged to produce the same weirdly high forehead and flattened ears. Now, that's the kind of thing you see only deep in the countryside. "Excuse me," she snaps, making John jump, but no, she's addressing her neighbour. "Your feathers are in my face."

The girl blows a smoke ring before saying, "You're welcome." Her French is thickly accented; that's about as much as this Irishman can tell.

"Take it off, why don't you?" the conehead demands.

"Hats go up in the ropes." Monsieur Dois points overhead helpfully.

"Not mine. It don't come off," the outrageous girl in orange claims. To John it sounds as if she's learned French only in recent years.

"Why not?" the conehead wants to know.

"It's sewn into my hair." Her poker face dares anyone to call her a liar.

Several passengers grunt or mutter. John finds it puzzling that none of them has raised any objection to the monkey.

The girl's not so much pretty as glamorous, he decides. Her figure's squat, her face spotty under its powder; she can't be eighteen, even. But she has a rueful insouciance worth more than beauty. She drops her cigarette stub on the floor, presses it with her high-heeled boot, and beckons to the coffee seller. "With milk."

The man moves the cup to the tap on his left—like a woman shifting her infant, John thinks, unsettled by the image—and releases a stream of white into the cup. "Fifteen centimes."

She makes a face. "I get a café au lait for ten centimes in Paris."

"Then wait seven hours," the coffee seller suggests cordially.

She sighs, fishes the coins out of a little bag dangling from her wrist.

"Dates, nuts?" he offers.

"Sugar."

"One centime more." He produces a lump from the folds of his robe and a tiny spoon on another delicate chain to stir it in.

The Frenchman called Dois looks up from his newspaper. "Did you sell coffee back in Africa?"

"No, monsieur, carpets."

A chuckle from Dois. He is clearly the sort of man who finds everything funny. John Synge is too solitary to manage that, but he appreciates the spirit.

The smoker swallows her first gulp with pleasure. "*Putain*, that's strong."

"Slow," the coffee seller advises. "Morning coffee is prayer."

"Is what?"

"You sit, sip little by little. Thank your god."

The girl smirks at that, suggesting she doesn't have one any more than John does since he threw away that crutch in his teens and broke his widowed mother's heart. "Any marc?"

John wonders if it might be against this man's religion to supply grape brandy.

But no, he's producing a bottle from his skirts. "Another ten centimes."

"I get a dash of marc for five in Paris," the plumed girl objects.

"Wait till Paris, then, dear lady."

With grudging respect for the coffee seller's bargaining, she hands over another coin.

He adds a slosh. "Pastry?" He holds out a box of small, honeyed crescents.

The young woman tosses her head like a horse irritated by its plumed headdress. "That's all you'll get from me."

John breathes in the scent of the coffee, but he really mustn't buy any; he's already behind on the rent for his two rooms (only one of them furnished), and it's only the twenty-second of the month. Most days he gets by on bread and an egg and a cigarette, with the odd visit to a cookhouse for a slice of meat if he's feeling faint. He borrows library books that he forgets to read and wanders the Louvre for half-days at a time. Since at twenty-four he has no definite plan for his future and little prospect of being able to earn a living, it seems wisest to keep his habits modest.

He fingers the corner of his notebook. He'd like to draw the full sweep of the girl's extraordinary costume . . . but she's right across from him, so she'd see. If she can afford that hat, John imagines she could pay for a Second-Class fare, so why is she mucking in here with the hoi polloi? Maybe she was flush when she bought the bird-encrusted hat, but she's broke today, and she still has too much pride to sell it? Anyway, though her trade might be legal in live-and-let-live France, surely the respectable passengers in Second would give her the cold shoulder.

She must be far from home, a bright migrant creature storm-blown into these northern European climes. John hasn't come as far, but as a stranger in Paris too reticent to have made any real friends, he feels for her.

A pair of dandies on the other side of him with the un-mistakable air of students—one pale and weedy in pince-nez and a faded tailcoat and bowler that look as if he took them off an elderly corpse, the other East Asian with a natty velve-teen jacket and hat—are gulping their coffee with pleasure. John is rather less shy about striking up conversation with his own sex, so he asks them where they're enrolled.

"At the Colonial School by the Jardin du Luxembourg, being trained up to tyrannize over far-flung regions of the empire," says the French one ironically. He introduces him-self as Max Jacob. He seems to John too frail to tyrannize over so much as a village.

His friend turns out to be Cambodian with the wonder-ful moniker of Kiouaup, though John can't tell whether that's a first or last name. They share a room in a boardinghouse by the "Colo," sleeping in hammocks while they're saving up for beds.

"I stroll in the Luxembourg all the time," John confides, "in the Poets' Walk."

Max Jacob sighs: "In the deep shade of those trees!"

He nods. "Were you holidaying in Granville?"

"No, no," says Kiouaup in his perfect formal French, "one of our professors insists we visit large industrial concerns and write up reports on how well they are administered."

John didn't realise Granville had any large industrial concerns. "A shipyard, was it?"

"*Merde*—quite literally," Max quips. "An awfully enterprising pair, the Dior cousins. They charge the townsfolk for emptying their toilets and sewers, then wave the magic wand of chemistry over the stuff and sell it back to the farmers as fertilizer."

He turns out to be a Breton. "We Jacobs are in the clothing trade—rather a cliché, I admit. We're the only Jews in Quimper."

John is impressed by this flippancy. Since the banishment of Captain Dreyfus for espionage, in April, it's a brave Hebrew who identifies himself as such in public.

A man who looks like a labourer hawks brown on the floor. Is this a hostile comment—could he be one of those ranters from the Antisemitic League? But it was John's old polished boot he just missed, so maybe it was just spit.

Max pays no attention. "Now, some say my family doesn't count because we're not *practicing*, but I say we don't need to practice—we've been at it for three thousand years."

This punch line makes John laugh. He wonders what it had been like for the young eccentric to grow up in a Breton provincial town. He remembers his own long, lethargic summers by the sea in County Wicklow, Mama never allowing him to swim on account of his weak lungs.

She'd call a Third-Class carriage a hotbed of infection, which it probably is. But John Synge hasn't yet discovered a way to study his fellow human beings at close quarters without breathing the same air.

"English, are you, *mister*?" That's the fellow called Dois asking Synge with a touch of mockery.

"No!" John's French grammar is basically sound, but he knows his pronunciation attracts attention. "Irish." That comes out too combative, but he simply loathes being mistaken for a member of the nation that has kept his own in chains.

Dois nods equably. "My own parents came from Portugal, but there are so many Italians in France these days, I'm often mistaken for one of them."

"Oh, yes?" John asks.

A half-chuckle. "After that anarchist baker from Milan stabbed President Carnot"—the conehead sighs at that and makes a sign of the cross on her chest—"my delicatessen got smashed and looted."

John is shaken by how lightly Dois recounts his persecution. How cruel the mob is, and how blundering. He thinks of the baker turned assassin; part of what's drawn John to Paris is its cast of radicals with their fascinating variety of proposals for remaking civilisation on fresh principles, and he'd describe himself as a socialist, but as for anarchism, he's sat through two lectures on the subject, and it seems madness to him.

The coffee seller leans back, resting the weight of the tank on its stick behind him. Does the fellow have to stand for the next hour or more? John murmurs, "Would you care to sit?"

"Can't, monsieur."

"Oh, the tank doesn't . . . it's not possible to set it down? That must be a nuisance."

The coffee seller shrugs, philosophical.

John shuts his notebook and stands up anyway to stretch his legs. It's already getting stuffy in this crowded carriage. He steps over the brown spit and inches around the coffee seller to pull up the window's belt and let it down a notch. He waits to see whether anybody objects. When he returns to his space on the bench, it's narrowed by several inches.

"What's that?" The plumed girl's question startles him. "What you putting in your little book?"

His fingers curl over its spine. "Just, ah, notes, mademoiselle." The words come out with a hitch and a slight wheeze.

"I go by Anna Lamor," she volunteers. "My stage name."

So she's a dancer or actress; that doesn't mean she's not a prostitute too.

"Anna with an *h*."

Synge smiles but doesn't follow. "Hanna?"

She shakes her head. "*H* at the end." She scratches her monkey's whorled head, no bigger than a large walnut shell.

Funny that, to insist on a silent letter in a made-up sobriquet. Is she trying to make it harder to spell? John tries again: "Annah."

She nods as if she hears the *h* this time. "Annah Lamor. *Lamor* sounds like love and death both."

42

L'amour, love, and *la mort*, death. "Very clever."

She's not propositioning him, is she? Just making conversation? Years ago John resolved never to marry and risk passing on his weak constitution to any children. But that hasn't freed him from the thrall of women. Sometimes the intensity of his response to their charms makes him tremble.

He pushes himself on. "So you're a performer, Mademoiselle Lamor?"

"Call me Annah."

"It seems stage names are the rule these days—Nini-Legs-Up, Glutton, Gelignite . . ." He's trying for the tone of a habitué of cabarets, even though he can rarely afford so much as a concert.

A shrug from Annah. "It's not a rule, just chic."

But chic would be a rule in her set, John guesses. The truth is, he spends most evenings walking around, mostly to save on heating his room. Not a boulevardier seen at parties so much a flaneur who wanders past and hears their distant music. He loves the night-hushed backstreets of Paris; he makes notes on the flutter of moths around a gas lamp, the skitter of a rat, the hoot of an owl.

"These *notes* in your little book—notes of music?"

"No, no." John tries to recall the last thing he was writing before getting on the train, or at least the last thing that wasn't some feeble sentence about the parabola of a woman's hem. "I've been, ah, looking into the folklore of Normandy. Sayings, stories . . . fairy stones and devil's bridges, that sort of thing."

Annah Lamor fixes her bold gaze on him. "Tell us a story, then."

"Ah ..." John stammers: "A, a story from Ireland?"

She jerks her thumb over her shoulder in the direction from which they've come. "Normandy!"

"Oh, right, Normandy, yes. Shall I?" He flicks through his jottings in a sweat. Is everyone in this crowd listening? Yes. (Well, probably not the conehead woman, who's now trying to persuade the mewling baby under her shawl to settle onto her breast.) "I did pick up a legend about the Normans attacking the Château of Pirou. Which was held by the English during that era," he puts in because otherwise the story makes no sense. Though how can he expect the young traveller from the Far East to know what era he means?

The man who spat on the floor before does it again now. Is he expressing scorn for the English this time? Or is he just suffering from catarrh?

John blunders on: "Probably the twelfth century."

Annah makes a get-on-with-it gesture, her feathers dancing. "They attack this château?"

"Yes, the Norman soldiers burst in, but all they found was one bedridden old Englishman—a wizard. He showed them his book of spells and informed them triumphantly that he'd just turned his lord and all the guards into wild geese—to let them escape, you see? But the attackers burnt the castle to the ground, and the wizard with it." Spoken aloud, the story sounds savage, bizarre. "And for want of that spell book to bring them back, the English lord and his men were condemned to fly round Normandy in feathered form forever."

The young woman's face splits in a grin, and now she looks barely fifteen. "Poor *connards*."

"Well, yes." John manages to smile back.

On the overstuffed crimson seat in her carpeted First-Class carriage, Marcelle de Heredia gazes out at the passing countryside. A brown mare with her foal. Two donkeys. Black-and-white cows trampling the ground to mud around a pond of geese. The wafting smell of dung. Marcelle's trying to recall the details of an article by a geologist arguing that *Homo sapiens* could have walked dry-shod from Normandy to Dorset. Or dry-footed, at least; she doubts cavemen had shoes.

A railway carriage is as intimate as a dinner party, but one with no host and guests assembled at random. Marcelle is sitting in a velvet, teak, and iron cigar box—thick carpet underfoot, heavy lace-edge curtains, the door rimmed with gilt Morocco leather—cheek by jowl with four strangers. She'd actually get more space to herself in Second, since it's less popular, but Papa would be horrified. (Having come from Cuba as a boy and then been subjected to so much insult in the National Assembly here, Papa always quietly insists on upholding his and his family's hard-earned social position.)

The red-cheeked industrialist opposite her has introduced himself as Émile Levassor. The wife (who uses both her husbands' names, going by Sarazin-Levassor) is splendid in a chartreuse travelling costume with dangling earrings. Marcelle, feeling rather underdressed in her tailored navy-blue outfit, is horrified to see that each earring is made of the head of a hummingbird. The girl, Jeanne, tucked beside her mother, is peeping at the glossy wooden hand of the dapper little silver-haired man in the other corner—Bienvenüe, was that it? Jeanne has volunteered to Marcelle that she's seventeen, but she seems younger; she's pale and lovely in a curly grey astrakhan coat with coloured embroideries of foliage over the lambswool. She's clearly her stepfather's pet, though Levassor has mentioned his stepsons fondly too.

Despite what fairy tales teach about remarrying, Marcelle often finds that second marriages have this quality of relaxation about them, perhaps because the match is based on sounder judgement. Her own mother had already been widowed when she married Papa, at twenty-four; Marcelle supposes that after a loss, what matters is to push on.

She leans back, but the scarlet velvet against her head is unnervingly doughy. She straightens again and watches the names on little blue signboards whipping past: *Folligny, Saint-Aubin-des-Bois, Mesnil-Clinchamps.* Villages where Marcelle will never stop; other lives she might have lived.

A serious student, she doesn't move at the leisurely pace of most rich men's daughters. As a rule, the women at her school of medicine don't believe in taking holidays; they fear being seen as dilettantes if they're gone for a week. They worship a tutor of theirs, an austere Pole called Madame Curie, who lives in a sixth-floor flat without heat, light, or

piped water. Marcelle was impressed to hear from a class-
mate that this tutor wore a blue cotton dress to her own
wedding, spent the gift money on a pair of bicycles for herself and her scientist husband, and went straight back to the
lab afterwards.

Marcelle is aware that as well as her sex her colour may
count against her. A pair of twits in her anatomy class once
asked her to settle a bet as to whether she was a quadroon or
an octoroon. She tries to shut her eyes to race hatred, given
that there's nothing she can do about it but submit work so
strong that no one can possibly argue that the daughter of
the famous Cuban doesn't belong at the school of medicine.

She has to admit that her week away from her studies
has been a tonic. Those cliffs yesterday evening! Marcelle
was on narrow rue de l'Égout, Granville's steepest staircase,
descending to catch the lemon-yellow October sunset over
the Manche, that sleeve of salt Atlantic between France
and England. The wind was in her face, so strong that she
could lean on it as if on an invisible wall. The lacy, glittering
sea was turning her thoughts towards her brother—his last
childhood holiday, thirteen years ago—and perhaps that distracted her because when the wind whirled around without
warning, Marcelle was suddenly sliding and skidding down
the hill, bumping over hard hummocks, yelping with fright,
trying to remember how far out the tide was and whether she
was likely to plummet onto rocks or into the water—

But she grasped long grass and lichen and finally ground
to a halt. Her skirt was torn; her legs were bruised.

Marcelle can never tell her parents about the near miss; she's the only child they have left, even if, at twenty-two, she's no longer a child. What a foolish way it would have been to lose her life. But the fall left her feeling oddly exhilarated.

Only yesterday, and her palms are still rough with scratches, but it seems like weeks ago. Marcelle's ready to get back to work—this minute, in fact; if she had the carriage to herself, she'd pull her typewriter (the best thing her father has ever bought her) out of its case. However, she can't face the raised eyebrows of elegant Madame Sarazin-Levassor. It draws attention if a lady does anything other than knit or embroider.

Émile Levassor grins across the car as if reading her mind. "Sorry to crowd you so, mademoiselle. The trains are so popular these days, we must put up with being shipped about like parcels."

Marcelle rouses herself to make chitchat. "You're not fond of the railway, monsieur?"

"Oh, it gets me to the general vicinity of where I'm going, but I'd rather steer myself right to the spot."

"My husband drives automobiles," Louise Sarazin-Levassor explains.

"Electric?" Marcelle asks with interest. Now that her father's retired from the National Assembly, he's been investing in those; *the way of the future*, he calls them.

Levassor shakes his head. "Internal combustion."

"And Papa designs and races his cars too," the girl boasts. Two spots of colour on her cheeks.

He laughs that off. "Well, mostly I sell them."

"He won a race in June—down to Bordeaux and back at an average of twenty-five kilometres per hour!"

"Came in first but didn't win," he corrects his stepdaughter, "as the race was meant for four-seaters and mine has only two."

"That's only a technique—technic—"

"Technicality," murmurs the wife.

"He drove it solo for forty-eight hours and forty-eight minutes," Jeanne says, "and the next car didn't show up for more than five *hours*."

The other man, Monsieur Bienvenüe, blinks up from his copy of *Le Figaro*. "Forty-eight hours and forty-eight minutes, really?"

"Mm, the figure's suspiciously neat," Louise Sarazin-Levassor agrees. "Darling, are you sure you didn't reach Paris five minutes earlier and drive around in circles till you got to forty-eight hours and forty-eight minutes exactly?"

Levassor pantomimes outrage. "Believe me, I'd have been prouder to come in earlier."

Marcelle is enjoying this family. "Did that include breaks to sleep?"

"Only catnaps on the steering wheel."

"A few breaks to dine, *bien sûr*," his wife says teasingly.

Jeanne's giggle turns into a cough.

Her mother buttons up the sable collar on the girl's coat and kisses her creamy cheek. "In ten years, everyone will have a motorcar."

"And we'll have to eat all the horses, I suppose," Levassor says.

This raises a general laugh.

"Never the dogs, though," Jeanne protests, rubbing her spaniel's ears.

"If I may—that would seem a rather horrid prospect." That's Bienvenüe.

"Oh, Papa didn't mean it, monsieur," Jeanne assures the old man. "He loves all animals."

"No, no, I mean the traffic jams that would occur if every man were really to have his own automobile. The stink of petrol, for one thing."

"It could hardly be worse than the pong of dung on the roads," Levassor jokes. "But no, I much prefer to drive in the countryside rather than in Paris—setting my own pace."

His wife pokes him. "Meaning as fast as the engine will go!"

He shrugs. "What can I say, *ma chère?* Speed is the only new pleasure invented since the ancients. The thrill of danger, the rush in the veins . . ."

Marcelle's heard men talk with such zest about love but not about motion.

"Skiing down an Alp, say," he goes on. "Your body feels on the brink of death, yet you're laughing!"

She wonders how that might work in terms of nerve response; how does the brain countermand the false reports?

Louise Sarazin-Levassor gives a shudder that makes her beaked earrings peck at the air. "I'd rather my body and brain were both quite clear on that point."

"But if I may say, in favour of the railways"—Bienvenüe, in his thoughtful tone—"they democratize that pleasure."

Democratize; Marcelle likes the word.

Just then there's a jolt, and Jeanne yelps.

"Merely going over a set of points," the little man reassures her. "The Company of the West really should replace its rolling stock, but it's in constant deficit due to all those underused branch lines in the western wilds."

"You're well informed, monsieur," Louise Sarazin-Levassor tells him.

"Well, I hope so, as my job is engineer in chief for bridges and roads, and that includes railways."

The Levassors murmur, impressed.

Engineer in chief, Marcelle thinks—meaning for the whole of France. She looks at the man's lapel and sees that of course he's wearing the red rosette of the Legion of Honour, the insignia of important men, like her mother's lawyer father. The one her papa would surely have been granted long ago if he'd been white enough.

The girl's eyes are glued to Bienvenüe's polished wooden prosthesis.

He smiles and extends it. "The railway took my arm—I was inspecting a train when I was so clumsy as to fall under its wheels." The girl leans in, avid to see how it straps on at the elbow. "I have another in my study with spread fingers and grippers."

"I wonder, monsieur, have you tried a typewriter?" Marcelle asks.

Bienvenüe nods, eager. "High-speed transport for the fingers, I call it."

"Your accident hasn't turned you against the business, then," Louise Sarazin-Levassor marvels.

His smile is rueful. "If it were asked of me, madame, I'd give a great deal more than one arm."

Like a zealot, this old gentleman seems willing to offer himself piece by piece. Marcelle thinks of herself as dedicated to science, but if it came to it, how much would she sacrifice for it?

As Jeanne picks up her spaniel for a cuddle, Marcelle catches sight of a purple smudge on the girl's inner arm. Only a tiny thing, but along with the other signs of frailty, it disturbs her.

The Levassors are asking Bienvenüe's advice about their eldest son's studies, so Marcelle takes the opportunity to talk to the daughter. She begins by admiring Ouah-Ouah, then slips in, "Did he nip your wrist there?"

Jeanne pulls down the lace of her cuff, sheepish. "Oh, I seem to bruise at the slightest touch."

"Has your mother tried arnica on them?"

She wrinkles her perfect nose. "Yes, but I don't like the smell. She fusses so."

"It's natural that she would, especially if . . . you've not been well?"

"Just tired, really." A shiver.

"Little appetite, I suppose," Marcelle suggests.

Another grimace from Jeanne. "They say I need bolstering,

so Cook serves me horse soup. Steak tartare in puddles of blood."

Who's *they*? Specialists, the family doctor, or just Maman and Cook? Sometimes people are too close to something to see it. Remorseless, Marcelle's mind is compiling the list: *chilly, thin, pale as paper despite an iron-rich diet, bruises easily*..."I wonder whether your gums bleed at all?"

Wide-eyed: "Only when I brush my teeth."

"And nosebleeds?"

"They're such a nuisance!"

Merde. Marcelle lets out the curse word in the silence of her head.

"However did you guess that, mademoiselle?" Jeanne asks.

"Ah, I'm studying medicine in Paris."

"You must be awfully clever."

Marcelle smiles, troubled. "And—if I may—do you ever wake up in a sweat?"

"Only because Maman insists on giving me too many blankets," Jeanne assures her.

No, no, no. Marcelle's suspecting the worst now. But of course, she may be jumping to conclusions.

Jeanne's looking at her with frank interest. "Were you delicate too when you were a girl?"

Marcelle hedges: "Perhaps a little." Her head's begun to hammer. She changes the subject to dogs and the particular charms of Ouah-Ouah.

In Rear Third, Maurice Marland is pressed tight between passengers, and his eyes are stinging from the smoke. (Though it's really no worse than the little house in Falaise when Papa and Georges have their pipes out.) On Maurice's left is an old man in a clerical collar who told him to sit down as soon as the train started to move. On his right is the solidly built young woman with short hair who jumped on just as the guards' whistles were sounding; Maurice thought she was a young man until his eyes went down as far as her skirt.

A grey-haired woman behind him is speaking Norman, the dialect of his dead grandparents. From schoolmates he's picked up enough to follow, but Maman says only proper French will help her sons get ahead.

Maurice has counted eleven heads in the carriage, including his own. He squeezes his shoulder blades together to occupy a little less of the hard bench. He should have taken off his school satchel, but there isn't room to do it now. If the carriage stays this packed, will he have to wear it till Dreux, five and a half hours away? For all the crush of bodies, the cold whistling up through the floorboards is making him shiver. He doesn't remember the inside of a train feeling so outside-ish, but of course his previous journeys were in the summer. Or maybe it's because he's by himself this time, and a lone traveller feels every draught.

"All on your own, *mon petit?*"

"No," Maurice lies, squinting at the priest in the clerical collar. Then he says "Father," for courtesy, though the Marlands, like many French families, aren't churchgoers the way their forebears were. He adds, "My parents are in the next carriage."

The truth is, they're in Dreux-don't-forget, where Papa will be outside the station at 2:20 this afternoon; he won't be able to come inside because a thief might drive his cart away. But Maurice doesn't want to call attention to the fact that he has no adult here to protect him.

The priest tips his wattled head to one side.

"It was too full in that carriage, so . . ."

"Fuller than this one, really?"

"Bursting."

The wrinkled mouth twists. "Ah, well, we all travel under Saint Christopher's care."

Maurice hasn't heard of Saint Christopher but does like the notion of a designated saint in charge of travellers.

He lifts his chin to try to see past his fellow passengers. Interesting sights unspool outside the window. Cows—pale, black-and-white, brown—all of them in one field lying down, all of them in the next standing up. (Could a noise have alarmed them?) A herd of shaggy sheep munching in a green lane so a gleaming coach-and-four can't pass; that's funny.

That peculiar young woman to his right is clutching the thin metal handle of her lidded lunch bucket so tightly that her knuckles are white. Maybe it's because she nearly missed the train at Granville; sometimes after the nervousness has worn off, you still feel sick. Maurice almost whispers it: "Was it the clocks, mademoiselle?"

"What?" Her voice is gruff.

He has to explain himself now. "Ah . . . I only wondered if you were confused by the clocks like I was."

"What clocks?" Deeper now, angry.

Maurice's face is scorching. "The one outside that's five minutes ahead. I mean, it's on time, but it's ahead of the one on the inside. To help passengers who are running late."

"I wasn't late," she mutters. "I just couldn't quite make up my mind to get on."

Maurice puzzles over that. When you're grown up, you have decisions to make, he supposes. At seven and a half, he has only instructions to follow.

"Of course all clocks are wrong," remarks the old priest.

"How's that?" Maurice forgets to say *Father* this time.

"Wrong by comparison with the celestial timepiece." The priest points his finger upwards; the end of it is flat and rather splayed.

A snort from the young woman with short hair.

Maurice guesses what timepiece the priest's talking about: "The sun?"

The priest nods. "By solar time, Granville is actually a full sixteen minutes behind our far-off capital, did you know that?"

Maurice shakes his head.

"But for the convenience of modern folk who like to gad about at top speed, we're obliged to deny the evidence of our senses and use so-called railway time, meaning Paris time."

"I'm still confused about the two clocks," Maurice confesses. "If you're a little bit late but they pretend you're not and hold the train so you don't miss it, won't you be late when you get off the train in Montparnasse?"

The priest nods, gratified. "They make this concession to their passengers' weakness, but like sin, it must be paid for sooner or later."

The young woman lets out a groan. "Did anyone here ask for a homily?"

A soldier agrees and says with a rattle of phlegm: "Hear, hear!"

But the grey-haired woman behind tuts at them loudly, and the priest gives her a civil nod. "I'm bringing my companion here to enrol at the Seminary of the Foreign Missions."

What companion? Maurice leans to see who's on the priest's other side—a young man whose face is cratered with old pimples.

The student missionary makes an awkward bow to the company. "I'm to travel on an ocean liner to Shanghai and convert the heathen."

The young woman laughs like a pistol shot. "What if they chop off your head?"

The missionary musters a lopsided half-smile. "There are the twelve martyrs of China already . . . so I suppose in that case I'd be the thirteenth."

He must be very brave, Maurice thinks. *Or very stupid. Or both?*

The old priest remarks in an oddly cheerful tone, "Martyrs may be made in France too. Didn't the Communards slaughter five holy fathers not a quarter century ago? And these days men of the cloth are being driven out of the schools so everything can be *secularized*."

The young woman grunts. "About time too!"

Maurice hates when grown-ups quarrel, so he looks out the window. He longs to shrug off his school satchel and relieve his aching shoulders. A tall, striped semaphore post bears a sign that says *One Train Can Hide Another.*

———

Mado Pelletier checks one last time that the lid of her lunch bucket is screwed on tight, then curls both hands around its handle again.

Mado is short for Madeleine, which is the name she chose for herself the day she decided never to go back to school. Legally she's still Anne, after her wretched mother, but Mado has shed that name along with the Good Lord and all that guff.

She wrinkles her nose; sweat, wet wool, garlic, and cabbage, reminiscent of home. She holds herself slightly away from the boy on her left, who's deep in a storybook. When she leapt into this carriage at the last minute, she didn't know it held any children. How is she supposed to think straight while she's right beside such a young one, today of all days? Well, she'll have to sit tight till the next stop, Vire. There's no way to get from one railway carriage to the next while the train is in motion, so each train car is a trap, albeit the sort people climb into willingly.

An arm's length away, a man with an angry-looking mole

on his nose is telling his neighbour about the past half-year of day-labouring. Neither of his two daughters looks more than ten years old, but the younger adds proudly, "We cleared stones off the fields and spread nightsoil."

"And now you're headed back to Belgium?" the brick-brown woman asks in a Breton accent. Her kerchief has slipped, showing cropped curls.

The hair harvesters must have been through her village recently, offering a yard of calico per head, Mado decides. *Vultures.* Mado's father used to say, *There's no end to the ways we get bought and sold, used and abused.* Paralysed by a stroke before she was born, Papa Pelletier was always in his chair in the corner, but he saw the world clearly enough.

"To my sister's house, yes," the labourer says. "And hope to return here next May."

His skinny girls cross themselves.

It never ceases to amaze Mado that so many of her ground-down sex still cling to piety, long after the majority of their menfolk have ditched it. She finds herself brooding over the plight of these Belgians, who'll make it back to Normandy in the spring only if that mole on the father's face doesn't spread and kill him. She wonders what got his wife, the children's mother. *Never mind, Mado. What difference do the specifics make?*

The tanned woman's telling the man that she's just given up farmwork herself, "seeing as the bastards keep cutting our wages and blaming it on the price of wheat."

Mado sighs. For every way the poor eke out a living, there's some sleight of hand by which the bosses make it harder or the landlords or big companies charge them more. Ever since Mado discovered the public library, she's been reading to learn how the machine of the world chugs on and how no fiddling little adjustments will ever fix it. When she came across Proudhon's *Property is theft*, the words went off like firecrackers in her brain.

"A cousin knows a soap works I can try in the city," the tanned woman goes on hopefully.

Mado's heart sinks for her. The city's already clogged with workers squeezed off the land who delude themselves into thinking they'll spot an opportunity somehow overlooked by all Parisians. She pictures this ruddy woman growing pale in a shed on the outskirts of the city, stirring chemicals with a wooden spoon.

The woman covers a small belch with her fist. Perhaps the motion of the train is upsetting her stomach. Or is her story more complicated—did some man let her down, and now she's a month or two gone, maybe, and headed for the anonymity of Paris to have herself discreetly "put straight"?

Mado digs her thumbnail into her finger. *Stop making up sad stories about these strangers. What difference does it make now?*

She feels the blood slide out into the roll of rags belted to her waist. Since Mado turned fifteen, she's bled every fourth Tuesday of the month, as if a weird clock in her belly keeps time. On the first occasion, the nun flushed red and sent her out of class for leaving a bright smear on the seat. At home behind the greengrocery, Madame Pelletier cleaned her daughter up without a word of explanation.

Mado has studied her mother's grotesque history and concluded that Nature's deck is stacked against females. Her mother had a healthy son, then two stillbirths, then Mado, then *ten* further misses, one after another—some who slid out in scarlet puddles, some quite well-formed infants who never drew breath. Whenever her mother's time arrived, she'd press the girl into service to assist the midwife. Nothing ever came of all that labour—no more little Pelletiers, nothing but stains on the floorboards.

Ever weeping, Madame Pelletier blamed the devil. But Papa taught Mado that her mother's losses and his own paralysis— such broken health among the hungry and worn out—could be no accident. Employers, politicians, and capitalists were to blame for the sufferings of the working classes. Pious royalist wife versus angry republican husband, the Pelletier marriage was a protracted war they waged in that stifling room behind the shop with Mado as witness. Papa gave up the argument by dying one night in his chair but not before he'd convinced his daughter that the system was rotten to the core.

Since walking out of school, Mado's tried dozens of ways to earn, each more hopeless than the last. Twenty-one already; she'd have left home by now, like her brother, no matter what the neighbours said if she could only find a line of work in which a young woman could earn as much as a man or even enough to pay her own rent. (Except *that* way; Mado would rather slit her throat than do that.)

"What's this getup for?"

Mado blinks, meets the eye of the farm woman. "I beg your pardon?"

"Why're you going around dressed like a boy?"

She's tempted to make a cutting remark about the woman's own hair, cropped to sell. Instead she answers flatly, "These aren't men's clothes, they're just sensible ones that keep the rain off." *Marks of liberty*, she'd say if it wouldn't cause general laughter. *A proclamation of the equal worth of my soul.*

"Well, they don't look like women's clothes."

Barely nine in the morning, and Mado's had enough of this day already. "They don't show my tits, you mean?" That makes a few eyebrows go up, though the old priest pretends not to hear. "I won't do that till men have to cut a hole in their trousers."

The tanned woman lets out a whoop. "I know a few dirty dogs who wouldn't mind that at all!"

A tiny voice makes Mado turn her head. *Merde*, here's another child right behind her—a girl in stiff new clothes playing some kind of finger game. Beside her, a woman with very different features and bags under her eyes; probably a nurse bringing her charge back to Paris. The bourgeoisie claim it's healthier for children to spend their first years in the countryside, but really they just prefer to pay their way out of any inconvenience, including child-rearing.

Mado's gorge rises. She doesn't want to know about the little girl or the nurse or any of these people whose knees are pushing against hers. Their muddy clogs, their stinks of sweat and sausage and tobacco. These people, her people—she's not naive about them. Their ignorance, their prejudices, the daily grind drags them down. *What does it matter who these particular individuals are?* Today's random selection from the millions of working folk who shell out far more than they can afford to be trucked along the rails of France like sheep to market.

The old priest makes the sign of the cross, and so does the spotty youth, which means the two of them must have glimpsed a spire in the green landscape flicking by. Mado despises their kind, the men who dose the poor with religion to keep them quiet.

She wishes she had a book to pass the time. Why didn't she pick up something from the woman at the stall in Granville? Then she rebukes herself for her weak impulse. The rich read on trains, escaping into made-up stories, having (they like to complain) *time to kill*. Don't they realise it's the other way around? The poor understand that old Father Time is killing all of us, little by little. Only those who work for a living understand the value of the limited time they're granted. They sell their portion by the hour or rest to gather their forces to do it all over again the next day. No, there's no novel that could distract Mado from reality now. She chants in her head, *I come of age today.*

The young missionary crosses himself again, which proves to Mado that he's a pious idiot because that last vertical was definitely a poplar.

Her satchel is digging into her hip. The uniformed veteran

beside her—blue-jawed, unshaven—rouses himself from his doze. "Bags off the seat." He doesn't even say *mademoiselle*.

She scowls. "This kid has one too."

The young boy blinks up at her.

"Put your schoolbag up in the net," the soldier orders the child. "We're packed like sardines here."

Mado considers defying him, but he doesn't seem the kind to back down. She lowers her lunch bucket and wedges it carefully between her feet. Then she stands up, pulls off her satchel, and nudges it into the overhead net, which looks on the verge of bursting. The Belgian labourer gets up to help. "I have it," Mado barks and almost stumbles as the train rounds a curve.

"All right, all right," the Belgian says.

Mado grabs the little boy's school satchel—the narrow straps are warm from his shoulders—and tosses it into the net. She has to get away from him, and from the small girl behind, and from the Belgian girls with cracked hands; these children are distracting her. How long till Vire now? She eyes the door. Young men have been known to dare each other to climb out of their carriage and—clinging to the rail, whipped by the wind—walk along the narrow footboard to the next. That's the kind of mischief Mado might have tried if she'd had the luck to be born a boy.

As soon as she sits down, she releases the grip of her feet on the lunch bucket, picks it up again, and holds it like a pet. Her treasure, her masterpiece, her beautiful bomb.

Since Granville, Engine 721 has been scenting danger some-where along her flanks. Sensing that this might very well be her last ride. Now she's tracked the evil to its source: this young woman in Rear Third.

You wonder how a train can read her passengers' minds? Consider the circumstances of her making. Iron ore (grey streaked with red) was drawn up from the veins of France and smelted to form gigantic plates. Forty-metre-tall teak trees in the Malay Peninsula were axed and toppled, chopped into logs, then planks, and shipped around India and through the Suez Canal. Of these precious stuffs, each of this train's parts was precisely and laboriously formed. On the day she was born, her noisy furnace heated up her boiler and brought her to panting life. But then came the true spark of creation: She was filled with people. Human beings, their damp hands, their endless chatter. Every day Engine 721 is sent hurtling back and forth across Normandy, gorging on characters of all kinds. They ride inside her, their wandering, wondering minds no less than their soft bodies. She savours their mem-ories and jokes, their doubts and rages, the way a worm tastes the earth.

And of all those who've travelled on this train over almost two decades, this awkward young person is the only one who's plotted her destruction.

Engine 721 doesn't take it personally. She is made of wood and metal, and her temperament is stoic. Besides, she recognises something kindred in Mado Pelletier's iron con-viction and unstoppable momentum. The bomber believes the world men have made is terrible, and so it is. Nor can the train deny that there is a certain beauty in the idea of burning, since she runs on flame herself.

That lunch bucket is an explosion waiting to happen. Its unstable elements sing out their longing so loudly, the train can hear them like a battle cry. All the force of combustion that makes an express the fastest vehicle on earth, this device has harnessed for instant havoc. It can take every part of an object, and every cell in the human body, and fire them in different directions.

So, for now, on we go.

9:59 a.m.
HALT VIRE

The most salient characteristic of life in this latter portion of the nineteenth century is speed.

W. R. GREG,
"LIFE AT HIGH PRESSURE" (1877)

Léon Mariette sits in his birdcage in the roof of Front Baggage. On this first leg from Granville, he's already checked all the labels and arranged trunks and valises by destination on shelves and in nets. He's read, absorbed, and filed in his pigeonholes the latest orders of service and memoranda from HQ. (Young Jean Le Goff may smirk at Léon's *officiousness*, but doesn't that word mean "zeal in performing one's duties of office"?)

Now the Paris Express is pulling into Vire, where this route crosses into Léon's home region, Calvados. How proud his meat-salter papa would have been to see him in a smart uniform with clean hands. The decaying town, known for its smoked sausage, sits on wooded slopes rising from the river, a factory chimney on one side, a clock tower and a ruin on the other. By the two-storey station, a couple of cabs are waiting, and people are standing about near the tracks.

As Pellerin slows the Express to a halt, Léon delicately applies his hand brake. One indecisive local scuttles across just in front of the train's nose. He shakes his head in exasperation; even when you build these fools a bridge or an underpass, they prefer to save half a minute by nipping across the rails. He glances over his shoulder to scan the eight passenger carriages behind. When a door starts to open, he peeps on his whistle and shouts, "Keep your seats till the train's come to a complete stop!"

The door is pulled to but not quite shut.

Passengers! He wishes he could lock them all in while the train's in motion. That used to be standard protocol—to stop anyone from falling out—but it's against the law since what happened in Meudon, on this very line just west of Paris. More than half a century ago, a train derailed there, and hundreds burnt alive in their locked carriages.

A final jerk now as Front Baggage's buffer bumps into the tender full of coal at 9:59, right on time; Léon stuffs his watch back into his fob as he clambers down three rungs into the van. A guard and his train are relay racers; while she's moving, he must wait, and only when she's at a standstill can he come to life. In Léon's mind, a ticking starts up like a deathwatch beetle. This halt is five minutes, fewer if possible, six at a pinch but not a minute longer.

"Vire," he calls as he jumps down onto the platform, "Vire Station." He grabs each of the pieces of baggage he's stacked ready on the floor of the van and passes it to a boy porter to prop on a waiting trolley. People rush the lad, snatching at handles. "Monsieur," Léon snaps at the first, "you're impeding the work."

Jean Le Goff's over on his right, slinging the valises of embarking passengers like sacks of turnips.

People are streaming off the train to find a water closet or buy wrinkled apples or pickled herring in newspaper from the woman with the basket. You'd think they've had a full day of travel already, rather than an hour and a half. If some of these time-wasters were considerate enough to keep their seats, it would be easier to see to those who required help, such as this conehead woman staggering down the steps of Middle Third with her arms full of bags as well as a large baby with a similarly modified skull. Léon snaps his fingers and directs a uniformed porter (hovering near a top hat, hoping for a tip) to her side. Sometimes the sheer number of people to be transported every day makes Léon's spirits quail.

There's a soldier carrying his kit out of Rear Third, and that crop-haired young woman with a lunch bucket right behind him. Neither of them heads into the station; are they thinking of sneaking into a Second-Class or even First-Class carriage while Léon's occupied?

No, the soldier's switching to Front Third, maybe because it's less crowded. The mannish girl does the same, but pauses on the step and calls out, "Guard?"

"What is it?"

"Parcels, Mariette," says a boy with a barrowful of goods to be shipped to Paris.

"Monsieur," Léon corrects him sharply, gesturing for the crumpled bundle of documents. It's 10:02 already. *Come on, come on.* If he ever falls down in an apoplectic fit, it'll be at a station in the last two minutes before the Express simply must depart.

"Any bigwigs riding with us today?" The crop-haired young woman is staring at the next two doors, the green ones.

Léon raises his eyes to heaven at her cheek. "Kindly take your seat!" Snapping his fingers to get the parcel boy's attention: "Get these trunks and valises into Front Baggage." Léon seizes the barrow himself and pushes it—*squeak, squeak*—one door down to the Post Van and starts loading parcels in by the armful.

For travel, Alice Guy wears one of the tailored suits she's had made for the office, a mauve one with a fitted jacket, great leg-of-mutton sleeves, and a skirt (made full by a bustle pad) that sways over her pointed boots. She hopes it's not too flattering but avoids actual dowdiness. Alice is twenty-two, and she's strikingly pretty, which is even more of a problem than her youth. When men come into Gaumont and Co., she does her best to discourage direct overtures, but a drip of flirtation is what oils the wheels of French life.

A step ahead of her, Monsieur Gaumont reaches for the handle of the first blue door.

He's clearly never given a moment's thought to the question of where a single woman and her married boss should sit on a train. If the two go together into an empty Second-Class carriage—apparently seeking privacy for the six hours back to Paris—how will that look to anyone who may glance in the window or get in at the next stop? If an acquaintance of Gaumont's glimpses him and his secretary in a tête-à-tête, Alice is the one who'll seem immoral, despite all she's done to ensure the respectability of this overnight trip to meet a photographic-lens supplier in Vire. All this flashes through her mind fast enough to make her murmur, before Gaumont even turns the handle, "Perhaps the next one, monsieur?"

"Really?" he asks blankly.

Is the idiot going to make her spell it out?

"As you like." Gaumont picks up their luggage and moves along the platform.

The next Second-Class carriage turns out to be already occupied by a dark man who smiles nervously with well-tended American teeth.

Gaumont stops short in the doorway and looks back. "Ah, mademoiselle, should we—"

"No, no"—Alice urges him in—"the whistle's about to go."

The American twitches, and for a moment she's afraid *he'll* offer to move to another carriage, leaving her and her employer alone after all.

Gaumont asks, "But wouldn't we be more comfortable in the first one?"

Alice restrains a sharp sigh. "This is fine." She takes a seat at the window opposite on the blue corduroy grudgingly stuffed with horsehair.

Her boss shrugs and puts their cases up in the net before he sits down across from her. He probably thinks her whimsical, arbitrary; an irrational female.

Alice nods to the other man, who wishes them good morning correctly but with a strong American accent. He turns out to be a painter. (Ever since that morning in Le Havre decades back when Monet daubed his first *Impression, Sunrise*, Normandy's been infested with painters.) Alice spent her childhood in Chile among people of all stripes, and she'd guess that most of this Henry Tanner's ancestors were African, though he's very light-skinned.

Gaumont casts a discontented look around. They're riding in Second less for comfort than to avoid the rowdy crowds in Third. Alice is sure he would travel in First if the firm could afford it. But she happens to know that Gaumont didn't grow up posh; he had to leave school at sixteen and work as a secretary in a precision-tools workshop. (At least he wouldn't have had her trouble with the gentleman customers.) He didn't buy the camera firm until this August, scraping the money together with the help of Monsieur Eiffel and two other investors. Word at the office is that the firm, Gaumont and Company, bears her boss's name only because

Eiffel's has been so unfairly stained by the scandal over the Panama Canal.

"May I have your notes to refresh my memory of the meeting, mademoiselle?"

"Of course." Alice opens her case, slides out the pages of specifications and prices in her neat writing—as unfeminine a hand as she can make it—and passes them over.

She was hired last year by the previous owner for her shorthand and typing (and, yes, perhaps for her Swiss-boarding-school polish). She had no knowledge of camera manufacture, but the business is oddly fascinating. In fact, there's something she wants to propose to Gaumont . . . but she hasn't found the right moment to broach the topic.

For now Alice buries herself in her novel, one of Zola's. Generally she enjoys stories about the railways—lovers just missing assignations or hurling themselves under the wheels. But this Zola book is verging on ludicrous, since virtually every character who sets eyes on a train seems to be driven to bloodshed as a result.

10:04 a.m.

DEPART VIRE

The arteries of iron
run through and renew
every part of the body
of this land, bearing life.

PIERRE LACHAMBEAUDIE,
"STEAM" (1846)

B lonska's knitting a sock, turning the toes as sharply as a driver steers a coach. She should finish this one before Flers and its mate by Surdon.

Her Third-Class carriage is crammed now; a North African with the most bizarre tank on his back, a soldier, a woman with the look of a domestic, a short-haired girl with a lunch bucket, and the moustachioed guard have all pressed in.

"*Quhwah*, ten centimes, only ten centimes."

"Not coffee?" the young woman asks the tank man, frowning.

"What we call it, yes, *quhwah*. Much stronger than your French coffee," he says with mild scorn. "*Quhwah* keeps awake, fixes bad stomach, headache, slow brain—"

"All right, all right," she says, "I'll take a cup."

"I've seen your discount pass before, Hakim," the guard remarks benignly, "no need to show me today."

Blonska doesn't see the *need* for him to expose the coffee man's poverty either.

Unable to bow due to his apparatus, Hakim dips his head and hastens to fill a cup for the guard; he gulps it and smacks his lips.

"I already ordered." The young woman sets her lunch bucket down between her feet with a tiny clang and puts out her hand.

"With milk? You want milk?"

"Only if it's still hot. Don't say it's hot if it's only luke-warm," she warns the coffee seller.

Hakim hesitates. "Milk is warm but maybe a little sour now?"

She curls her lip. "The coffee's still hot, though?"

"Yes, yes." He gives one of his chained cups a wipe with his sleeve and fills it for her. "Sugar, dates?"

The young woman shakes her head.

The smell is so rich and flavourful, it's making Blonska a little dizzy. But she hates to spend ten centimes for no good reason.

The guard wipes his moustache and asks for the short-haired girl's ticket. It seems the cardboard's not nipped as it should be.

"That's not my fault! They didn't touch it at Granville."

"True, their inspector's very slack. I saw you leg it in here at Vire," he teases. "What was wrong with Rear Third—someone let one rip and stank up the place?"

A couple of passengers grunt at his coarse humour. But Blonska's never minded frankness about bodily matters; the delicate proprieties of her patrons in Paris only amuse her.

"Too many priests in Rear Third," the young woman mutters.

"Ah, you have a point. Fleas on our backs, and why they still get a rail discount, I do not know." That bit the guard delivers under his breath—to avoid giving offence, Blonska supposes, as so many rural folk still cling to their beads.

Funnily enough, her patrons tend to assume she's pious—her bare-bones ways make no sense to them except as an imitation of the saints. Blonska lets them believe it, since belief consoles the believers.

Lacking such false comforts, she gets only the grim satisfaction of doing her best. She has a taste for helping, simple as that; it's meat and drink to her. For the rich ladies of her acquaintance, this Russian émigrée is an invaluable agent, a broker of their largesse. (They find her knowledge of literature impressive, her accent picturesque, her skewed frame poignant.) Blonska has no embarrassment about climbing staircases to mould-stained apartments where people need her and the linens and provisions she carries. She relishes dealing with intractable problems, calming drunken husbands, arguing with harsh landlords, even assisting with the occasional birth if the midwife's delayed. Above all, she never tries to cheat the poor with the spurious consolation of a *better life to come.* Without attempting to improve or uplift, Blonska doles out practical advice sparingly and francs by the fistful. She may be doing no good, of course; she knows the needy can sometimes be bewildered by too much hard cash. They get robbed or drink it and a week later are no better off or even worse. Still, it relieves her to give away that filthy lucre; she seems to step more lightly, breathe more easily afterwards.

Hakim is leaning back now, resting his weight on a stick at the rear of his tank. Oh, that gorgeous aroma. After Blonska's long night on the cold platform, she's feeling ragged; she may be in no state to walk to her room when she reaches Montparnasse late this afternoon. So she raises one finger in his direction and fumbles out a coin. She tucks her knitting back into her bag in case of a spill, and while she's at it, she gets out her brown ticket to show the guard. Sipping the lovely stuff, she reminds herself to make it last.

The woman at her left elbow, the one with the look of a maid, wants to know, "What brought you to France, then, Monsieur Hakim?"

Blonska bristles slightly on his behalf because although the woman's addressed the man politely, such a question is often a prelude to a rant about foreigners *feeding like rats in our larder.* At the very least it's a pointless query, because who can tell what brings anyone anywhere? What brought Blonska this far west? Paris is the centre of the literary world, but was that why? She has trouble remembering. Life has tides and currents that can wash a person up anywhere.

Hakim must be used to delivering his story along with the coffee. "I came from Algiers for six months only, to work in the souk in the Tunisian Pavilion."

The maid's face brightens. "Oh, the Expo! What fun."

Six years ago, Blonska remembers. She very much doubts Hakim found that job *fun*. "Why Tunisian, may I ask, if you're Algerian?"

"That was the name," Hakim says, "the Tunisian Pavilion in the Village des Noirs. Before, I sold carpets, but in Paris I was paid to sit on the floor."

"You weren't allowed a stool?" the young woman with the lunch bucket demands.

Blonska understands her anger. "They wanted you to squat so you would look more like an Arab?"

Hakim's eyebrows move as if he would shrug if his cumbersome apparatus allowed him.

"Why'd you switch from carpets to coffee?" the guard wants to know.

"More easy to carry than carpets."

It doesn't look easy to Blonska.

The maid takes out a book now. The title on the worn yellow jacket is *The She Devils*.

"A good read?" Blonska asks.

A pleasurable shudder. "Wonderful. This lady actually *eats* her lover's heart."

"My, my." The Russian's tastes run more in the direction of political history.

The woman introduces herself—Madame Baudin, a live-in on the rue de Rennes just a few minutes from the station in Montparnasse.

Blonska's lady patrons all share the fixed idea that Bretons make the most wholesome domestics; they'd never picture their maids reading stories of cannibals. Blonska gives her own name and origins in return. "But no one calls me Mademoiselle Blonska—I go by plain Blonska."

"I don't think I've ever met a Russian," Madame Baudin admits.

"Having a holiday in Vire?"

Madame Baudin shakes her head. "Connecting from Saint-Malo, where I was seeing my daughter yesterday evening."

"Just overnight?"

"My husband's valet to a gentleman off the Champs-Élysées. Till he and I can find jobs where we're allowed to live together, his mother's raising our Bleuenn. Such a size the girl is now!" A hitch in her voice.

Blonska flinches in sympathy. She wonders whether the child even knows her mother.

Across the carriage, the short-haired young woman keeps her eyes shut as if she's in pain.

Blonska murmurs, "He couldn't make the visit with you?"

"Our days off hardly ever fall together." Madame Baudin's tone is fatalistic, as if that's as much of a fact as the weather.

The short-haired girl tugs at her stiff collar and mutters, "How they stamp on our necks."

A shrug from Madame Baudin. She grins in Blonska's direction. "So angry, this one, so young!"

But Blonska can't disagree with the resentful girl. One of the chief indignities of the underclass is being at the mercy of employers who won't let you choose when to take the little time that's your own.

The soldier's halfway down a bottle of marc; he crosses his legs now, his boot almost knocking over Mado's lunch bucket.

She snatches it up, glaring.

"What's your name, dear?" Madame Baudin asks.

Mado hesitates, frowning. But it can do no harm to give it at this point. "Mado Pelletier."

"Hmm, I don't think I know any Pelletiers, but then, Paris is so vast, isn't it?"

Mado ignores the maid and tries to concentrate her mind on the First-Class carriage that's just behind this much-varnished wooden wall. First Class is always cushioned halfway along the string of carriages, since in the event of a crash, compensating even one wealthy family for injuries or death could well bankrupt the Company. This train is a moving image of the unfairness of the long con of life. But Mado is sitting so close to those important personages in First Class that if there were a knothole, she could peep through and catch a glimpse of black top hats and peacock silks. If only she knew exactly who's in there today.

She saw today's date on a poster about the opening of the new session of the National Assembly; she pictured them gathered in their half-domed chamber, the five-hundred-odd rich men who recently passed the brutal laws that locked people up for writing or shouting or even thinking *Long live anarchy.* These parasitical parliamentarians notorious for accepting bribes. And then a week ago, it occurred to her that on October 22, when the deputies converged on the capital from their country châteaux, most of them would take the train, faster and smoother than their coach-and-fours, if more public. Some of them might travel in before the opening, of course, but if Mado picked a morning express to Paris from any northern town on the twenty-second itself, surely there'd be a good chance of finding at least one of those cursed deputies on it?

She pictures an imaginary politician mere centimetres away behind the wall, unknowing. The face of a fop in a cartoon, with ostentatious whiskers. Oblivious to Mado and her astonishing lunch bucket.

Why has no one else in France thought of copying the Irish in London and setting off a bomb on a train? The six companies are owned by the state but privately operated, so every steam train roaring past represents government hand in glove with industry, turning the nation into one nightmarishly efficient factory to transport materials and workers and finished goods, thus maximising profits at the expense of the common people. What more obvious target could there be than an express, a symbol of so-called progress at its most ruthless?

When Mado hurried on at Granville, she was flustered enough to jump into the *rearmost* of the three Third-Class carriages, not remembering the importance of proximity to First Class. Also, it turned out to be full of children. (She puts their faces out of her mind.) This one, Front Third, is much better—and right beside the rear First-Class carriage so that any explosion here will surely rip that one apart too.

There's a game of dominoes going on in the corner now, on the back of someone's suitcase. A pack of cards is being shuffled for piquet. The soldier's filling his pipe. (Mado tells herself that he's probably fresh from firing on striking glass-makers or massacring the peasants of Madagascar.) He pulls out a little box that says *Double-Ended Safety Matches*, breaks one in half, and grates the two ends together to make a flame.

She allows herself a tiny smile. She put her device together only this morning, working meticulously but fast. The recipe's her own but based on tips from several dozen newspaper reports that she's gathered over the past year. She started with saltpetre and sugar. (*Enough to cure fifty kilos of ham*, she told the grocer in Granville.) A vial of sulfuric acid (*To take off obstinate corns*, Mado claimed) at one pharmacy; another of picric acid (*For burns*) at the rival pharmacy. One bag of nails, one of charcoal, and five boxes of the same matches as the soldier's, bought at three different hardware shops to avoid suspicion.

Back in her hotel room, Mado lined the base of her tin

lunch bucket with the nails, the simplest of projectiles. She snapped the flammable ends off the matches and ground them to grit with the heel of her shoe, then used the handle of her hairbrush to stir the grit carefully into the charcoal, saltpetre, and sugar. (Her breath coming loud and fast, as if she were running.) From each of the tiny vials, she poured off the acid's protective topping of water, then plugged it with cotton ripped off her hem and set it into the streaky mixture. Her lidded lunch bucket is now a reversal device, as foolproof as an hourglass. As soon as it's turned upside down, the acids will eat away at the cotton plugs, then drip into the dry mixture and set it alight. According to her research, her bomb should flare purple before it explodes.

Mado can't be sure how fast it will happen or how huge a blast it will make, but she knows it will be big. She'll embrace her clever creation, making an offering of herself.

An offering of all of them in this carriage, rather. This one will be the centre, the first blown to bits, and First Class and its fat cats will be next. Of course, most of these Third-Class passengers, considered as individuals, have done nothing to deserve their fate—the fisherwoman lugging her oysters, the Russian with her twisted back, the maid who's missing her daughter, the Algerian staggering under the weight of his coffee tank . . .

But think of all the others. The ones not on the train because they can't afford a nine-franc ticket—the silent majority. Men and women and children sowing, reaping, threshing, sawing, and fetching water, never going anywhere, never at rest. Not to mention the half-size, the hunchbacks, the club-footed, sufferers from goitre or scrofula, herniated woodsmen and blinded stonebreakers, the people racked with dysentery or coughing up bits of lung. Crews of children sent off after harvest to trudge ten days to the capital and somehow scrape out a living there. Sweeps, bootblacks, organ-grinders, rouged boys euphemistically called Little Jesuses standing on corners. (Mado once met a child whose parents had sold him into the trade on the promise of fifty francs for the year; he'd caught syphilis by Christmas.) *I'm doing this for all of them,* she reminds herself furiously. *Because there's no cure but revolution. Because what else can I do?*

She's curiously breathless. Time—her final stretch of hours and minutes—is speeding up. For years her dull, arduous youth has dragged past, but today it surges like a river in spate. She doesn't know exactly when she's going to turn her lunch bucket upside down, but she'd like to wait for the train to fill up in hopes of taking a member of that damnable parliament with her. In any case, the perfect moment will be sometime in the next six hours, between now and 3:55, when the Express is due at Paris-Montparnasse. Each minute feels large and vivid, illuminated by a spotlight but rocketing past, impossible to catch.

Mado did think of leaving a note in her hotel room this morning justifying herself. She'd have rather liked to write a manifesto eloquent enough to change the hearts of everyone who read it. The way Émile Henry's burning eyes had changed her last year.

Even before the young dynamitard threw that bomb into the café at Saint-Lazare Station, Mado was in sympathy with the cause. That came of her eating up everything she could find in the library but also posters, graffiti, reading Paris itself like a great stained volume of exploited lives. She hovered at the back of meetings; picked up songs in smoky cabarets:

Long ring the explosion's blast—
Let everything smash!

That's what made Mado get up at half past three in the morning to attend Émile Henry's execution outside the Grande Roquette prison, where four hundred troops held back the crowd with bayonets. The bomber was only twenty-one, and when he shouted, *Vive l'anarchie!,* across a hundred metres his beautiful dark eyes locked onto Mado's. As the guillotine's blade dropped, some spark leapt between them—that's the only way she can explain it. As if a torch dropped from his hand and it was she who snatched it up.

But no, Mado's no good at writing manifestos, and she's decided it'll create more widespread terror if her great gesture speaks mutely, anonymously. Which means her name will likely be left out of the reports of the disaster that will wing their way around the earth tonight. Very well; there's nothing particularly special about Mado Pelletier's story of growing up poor and raging. All she can hope is that the flames she's going to ignite will join with others being lit all over the world to bring the whole crumbling edifice down.

From each according to his ability—that's what Marx teaches, and this is Mado's ability: She's a realist who can see through the lies. Including the lies that revolutionaries tell themselves. There've been many thrilling attacks in France in recent years, but to Mado's mind, not one of them has been big enough. Young Émile Henry was the bravest; still, his bombs killed only one in the railway café and five at the mining company. Caserio's knifing of the president, though a great coup, still took down only one man. Neither the famous Ravachol's little devices nor Vaillant's nail bomb in the Chamber of Deputies managed to do more than injure a few people. No, the way Mado sees it, what's needed is one act of violence too spectacular to ignore. Hundreds must die at one go, and they must include someone deemed *important* so the attack will hit the headlines all across the world.

She's plotted alone, as anarchists generally do; telling no one is the only sure way to keep a secret. Anyway, the other self-proclaimed diehards would likely only scoff at the plans of a *girl*.

After Mado blows up this train, two things should follow. She corrects herself—*will* follow. The powers that be will know that nowhere is safe. The ministers of state, the generals, the factory-owners, the landlords, the speculators— let them shiver. The smug bourgeoisie, the idle boulevardiers who stroll along their horse-chestnut-lined avenues from one gleaming café to the next—they'll be put on notice that as long they oppress the poor, vengeance will stalk them. And even more crucially, the downtrodden will glimpse the weakness of those who've kept them underfoot for so long and feel their own force so that maybe not tomorrow or the next day but sooner or later, they'll rise up and topple this regime, clearing the way for a better one.

"Coffee makes my hands tremble," murmurs the Russian, shaking them like wet rags. "Still, I do feel stronger." She passes her chained cup back to Hakim, and he cleans out the grounds with a rag.

Mado lets out a long breath. Maybe she should have detonated her device the minute she got on the train at Granville, even without any guarantee that a deputy or another important man is on the Express. Because the one flaw in her plan is that riding for hours in Third Class means getting familiar with these people before she has to kill them. Of course Mado has qualms; only the icy-hearted would have none.

The Paris Express rushes into fog. A signal lamp in the safe position—tilted diagonally—glows green through the translucent grey of the woods. A nearby village is ringing its bells to guide any travellers who might have lost their way. Guillaume Pellerin's grateful for the headlamp burning at his engine's nose. Even if its white light, multiplied by reflectors, is not enough to illuminate what's ahead in time for him to stop, at least it could warn a child or a cow of the train's approach, surely?

Guillaume has no memory of choosing this trade, which

was his father's. But having given the Company half his thirty-five years so far, he has no particular complaints. It's a hard job, and only hard men can do it, which is why drivers get such respect. He's holding up all right, just a touch of rheumatics in the legs and occasional numbness in the right foot. His heart ricochets under stress, which he's mentioned to no one, not even his wife, Françoise, or Victor Garnier here by his side; Guillaume just stays quiet till the sensation wears off.

For a while now he's been qualified to apply for promotion to under-chief of a station workshop, but the truth is, without Engine 721 thrumming below his boots, he'd be as clumsy and restless as a sailor on dry land. Even now, on Guillaume's days off, when he leaves his watch on his dresser and drifts through the day waiting for Françoise to ask him for favours or call him to meals—what he could never tell her is that he misses being on the rails.

He remembers dandling baby Guillaume for hours, swimming in that bubble of timelessness in which infants float. But at ten, the boy is chafing, saying he wants to be a driver *now*. The Company might give him a scholarship, then take him as an apprentice as early as twelve. That way, three Guillaume Pellerins (grandfather, father, and son) will form a chain of generations in the service before they all lie down in the same plot in the cemetery, just a stone's throw from Montparnasse Station.

Through his goggles Guillaume catches sight of a dark print of pine on the brow of a distant hill. So many different trees whipping by. October gold showing amid the emerald and rust where a beech hedge is beginning to turn. A double row of poplars already stripped bare by autumn, huge balls of mistletoe standing out in their narrow crowns. A lone leaf gatherer hurries out of the woods with two sacks, illicitly harvested.

Guillaume returns his gaze to his controls, fingering them delicately. A driver intimate with his route will lengthen the pistons' travel to boost the torque before an upgrade, then shorten them to put on a burst of power. He's been trained to keep his hands off both the powerful air brake and the weaker shoe brake because having to brake is an admission of failure and means you're going too fast. The best way to control speed is with the reverser. Keep the regulator open but move the reverser closer to its midpoint between forward and back, which will reduce the cutoff, the moment in each stroke when no more steam is let into the cylinders, thus leaving room for the steam to expand. The Company notch, rollers call that magic midpoint at which the train runs with enough power but burns the minimum of coal. Guillaume clings to that notch in hopes of making the maximum bonus for savings on fuel and lubricants. Not that he or Victor can predict exactly how the sum will work out once the clerks in HQ scrutinize the logs and pass judgement, but surely one of these months, Engine 721's rollers will get their full bonus of forty percent?

Oh, but she's a good beast, leaning into the curves and racing along each downgrade. Guillaume feels her power thrilling in his own limbs, her sleek precision. As if she and he and Victor are one hybrid creation, a mixture of human and machine, like an iron spear hurtling across Normandy.

To a trackman in the ditch, one of his trouser legs ending in a peg, Guillaume lifts a chilly hand in greeting. The track-man was probably train crew till an accident maimed him. Such a quiet job that must be, inching along the rails, giving a hammer tap to every oaken sleeper that holds them up, and listening for any sound of hollowness or rot. Guillaume's glad he himself never has to work alone.

Coming into Orne Department now, and the line's slant-ing southwest. In front of a guardhouse, a broad-shouldered gatekeeper in her flat hat and red-and-white-striped skirt brandishes a red flag at the impatient farmers with the carts behind the barrier. As good a moment as any for Guillaume to test the air brake by nudging the valve handle a little open, which he likes to do early in each journey, even though the Westinghouse system is infallible. A driver or a stoker can apply the brake up here, but so can the guards in front of and behind the passenger carriages. The Westinghouse fail-safe design guarantees that if anything cuts the air line—if a great tree suddenly falls across the train, say—the brake automatically comes on.

Once the engine is past the crossing, running hard again with regulator open to the full hundred and eighty degrees, Guillaume allows plenty of steam into the cylinders. Every minute or so he grabs the rail on his right with his left hand and swings out far enough to check if the side rods are still going up and down, because if they look stationary, that's a sign of moving too fast. For want of any measuring device that shows the train's speed, this is the trick every driver knows, and it takes far less time than counting telegraph poles. Guillaume also keeps an ear out for any change in the cadence of the rail joints clicking under the wheels or in Engine 721 herself, her whistling breath.

As Guillaume straightens up, Victor catches his eye and nods: *All right.* Like sailors in a perpetual hurricane, they inch around each other in a pas de deux.

Jeanne Sarazin-Levassor has settled back against her mother's right shoulder and fallen into a doze. Louise leans into her, sets her cheek against her daughter's, too softly to rouse her. She particularly loves the girl's right ear, which sticks out a bit more than the left, turning flame red when the sun shines through it.

This child of seventeen is spun from Louise's silk, baked in her oven. The eldest of her babies but the only one close at hand, since she's had to let René (just seven!) go off to school with Auguste-Henri, meaning Jeanne is in some sense her last baby as well as her first. Jeanne's the best for cuddling; tactful of limb, always tucking in just so, never flailing or twitching or awkwardly elbowing. Almost grown up, she still loves to be held and patted and kissed, especially recently.

A secret of mothers: We enjoy it when our offspring are under the weather because it draws them back to us again, reverses time a bit, spins the hands anticlockwise. For a little while they need us as they once did every minute of the day, and we surrender reminiscently to that sweet rush.

Jeanne wasn't always easy in her younger years, squabbling with Auguste-Henri ... but these days she's always saying thank you in her soft breathy voice. Always resting her head on whatever piece of Louise she can reach. What Louise would never say to Émile—and never said to her first husband, Édouard—is that the caress of a lover can't compare to the touch of your child.

One of these years Jeanne will get married, Louise lectures herself. You must let your young grow up, move away from you, settle perhaps a great distance from Paris. Some greedy mothers do keep one girl home *to help*, but Louise wouldn't do that. The Sarazin-Levassor family head out into the world at cracking speed.

The one-armed engineer is waxing lyrical about public transport now; he calls it the greatest gift of modernity. "A train line to an isolated hamlet such as the one in Brittany where I grew up—it's like a lifeline thrown to a drowning man."

The foreign-looking student in the sober blue outfit, Mademoiselle de Heredia, says, "But monsieur, when you consider how many can't afford a ticket ..."

Bienvenüe nods soberly. "My hope is that the price can be brought down in time, as has happened with other innovations such as the post and the telegraph. We all benefit if goods and citizens are permitted to circulate like warm air passing through a room."

Which reminds Louise to wonder about the heater under

her daughter's feet. She can't move without disturbing Jeanne on her shoulder, so she gestures to her husband. Émile bends, feels it, and makes a face, which means it's barely lukewarm, for all the guard's promises. Louise points to the travel rug, and Émile hurries to unfold it over the girl's knees.

He's telling the engineer how they met—how Louise, carrying on her late husband's business of representing Daimler automobiles in France, licensed Émile a twin-cylinder engine, "and the next thing I knew, she was including herself in the contract!"

He's fond of that line. Louise gives him the indulgent smile he's expecting.

Bienvenüe is very curious about the car's design, so Émile gets out his portfolio, switches to the scarlet banquette beside the engineer, and spreads out the blueprint on his lap.

Mademoiselle de Heredia asks Louise if she might take Émile's seat beside her to admire the countryside to the north.

"Certainly." Making conversation, Louise tells her about a cooking demonstration put on last week by a lady who publishes a magazine called *La Cuisinière Cordon Bleu*. "*Cuisinière* as in 'woman chef'—a new notion to me! But she had a real chef there plying his skills, on an electric-powered stove, no less."

Mademoiselle de Heredia nods; she seems uninterested in gastronomy. Or in making the most of her looks, which are rather good, with a distinctly Mediterranean tint. "A lovely girl, your Jeanne."

"You're very kind." Louise rests her cheek again on the soft haze of her sleeping daughter's hair.

"I believe she hasn't been very well?"

"Oh, she's rather worn out from growing so fast. I tell her she wouldn't get so chilled if she'd eat more and put some padding on her bones!"

"No doubt."

But there is doubt in Mademoiselle de Heredia's voice; Louise can hear it.

"I do wonder . . ." The young woman is frowning a little now. "Has your doctor considered—has he mentioned anything about perhaps testing her blood?"

Testing for what? Louse pulls back—as much as she can, sitting practically pressed against this stranger, with Jeanne's sleeping weight on her other side. But she answers courteously. "Oh, I was rather anaemic too at her age, but I shook it off." Not spelling out what's understood, that a girl's monthlies can sap her powers.

"Mm."

"Greensickness, my mother used to call it. She always said the best cure was a husband, and I've had two, which may explain my excellent health!"

A nod from Mademoiselle de Heredia, as if she's reserving judgement.

Louise is nettled. Is this scientific young female one of the up-to-date kind who rail against marriage?

"It was actually a different test I was thinking of," the student says.

"Oh, yes?" Louise responds, just to be polite.

"For milkiness."

"My daughter hardly drinks milk at all. It turns her stomach. I can barely persuade her to take a little cheese after dinner."

"No, I didn't mean ... I'm referring to a special test of the blood. If it turns out to have a milky quality ..."

Louise's pulse is speeding up. She may not understand exactly what Mademoiselle de Heredia getting at, but the implication is clear: That Jeanne may be suffering from something serious, a mysterious disorder revealed by a *special test.* What a thing to suggest to a stranger on a train! On Louise's shoulder, the sleeping head is suddenly painfully heavy. Lowering her voice so the men won't hear, speaking almost into the young lady's ear: "My dear mademoiselle, you're not a physician?"

The dark eyes dull; the lovely face falls. "No, no."

"Are you advanced in training to become one?"

"Not really. My course of study—"

Louise cuts her off. "You have no qualifications to entitle you to make a diagnosis, then? Nor to speculate, nor interrogate me and my child in what I must say is a remarkably intrusive manner—"

"Madame, let me apologize." Which comes out high-pitched, and both men look up from their papers. Flushed, Mademoiselle de Heredia whispers: "I shouldn't have said anything."

Louise's rage, not easy to rouse, is not easy to soothe either. How dare this nobody try to fill her with obscure, nonsensical fears? "You're a stupid girl with notions, then. Showing off your brains," she says too quietly for the gentlemen to hear.

Without another word, the young woman goes back to her own seat, on the other side of Jeanne.

Her pulse loud in her throat, Louise fumbles for the *Cordon Bleu* magazine in her bag so she can pretend to read it.

———

To pass the time, Alice Guy is luring the reserved American out of his shell. It turns out Henry Tanner is not only a painter but an amateur photographer who always travels with a little camera of the "detective" kind.

"Disguised as a brown-paper parcel, is it?" Gaumont looks up at the baggage net.

"Disguised as a watch," Mr. Tanner corrects him in his stiff French. He pulls his watch out of his pocket and flips it open, which lets the hidden lens telescope out.

"Ingenious!" Alice leans in for a closer look. "So you can take pictures without attracting attention or alarming the subjects."

"Yes. Just to remind myself of the details of something I may want to paint later."

Alice sees an opening. "Monsieur Gaumont and I saw a terribly interesting demonstration at an industrial conference recently," she says. "These two brothers, they showed a film—" She breaks off, seeing in the American's eyes that he doesn't understand *film* in this new sense. "A series of photographs on a transparent strip of celluloid that are lit up and shown in rapid succession, you see, to form a scene?" She'll never forget the surprise of it. In that room full of scientists and moneymen, after a long morning of suppressing her yawns, she woke from her torpor with a jerk.

"The Lumière brothers are married to a pair of sisters," Gaumont mentions, "and the sisters' brother has married the Lumières' sister, would you believe."

Alice tries to keep on topic. "A moving picture, you follow, Monsieur Tanner? If a string of images is projected one after another fast enough, more than ten of them per second—"

"An illusion of motion is created?"

"Exactly! The eye is tricked. I should have known an artist would grasp it," she murmurs.

"Like a zoetrope. Or a ... in English we say *flip-book*." Mr. Tanner mimes flipping pages with his thumb.

"*Folioscope*, in French," Gaumont supplies. "But quicker, smoother."

"And what was the scene these Messieurs Lumière showed you?"

"That's an excellent question," Alice says, "because—"

But Gaumont cuts in. "Oh, it could have been anything, really. The technological innovation is the thing."

She sets her teeth. Any woman who works with men learns ways to avoid disagreeing head-on. "All the brothers did was set up their camera outside their own factory as the girls filed out after work. There was no art to it."

Gaumont shrugs. "I suppose the process could be used to record the movements of animals, wind, machines—anything scientific."

"But why scientific?" Alice hears her voice; lowers and

sweetens it. "I don't understand why a film *necessarily* needs to be a document of reality."

Her boss gives her one of his squints.

She adds, "Why limit it to a dull scene of tired workers walking by?"

"They've made other films. Apparently their next one's going to show a train coming into a station."

Alice spots an opening: "So could we! Make other films, I mean."

Gaumont frowns and turns back to the American. "Our firm's in the business of selling photographic equipment and supplies." As if he's enlisting this stranger's support against the silly secretary.

Alice smiles to soften her words. "We have those chronophotographic cameras you bought off poor bankrupt Demenÿ . . ." That was indiscreet; she shouldn't have said *bankrupt* in front of someone who—it occurs to her—may be a potential customer. "We actually brought one with us to Vire, Mr. Tanner, as our lens supplier was curious to see it."

The American picks up the hint, follows her eyes to the polished wooden case in the overhead net. "Really? Might I . . ."

"Of course."

She starts to get up, which obliges Gaumont to leap up and lift the camera down with both hands. "Our engineers are still tinkering with the design," he warns, sheepish about the cumbersomeness of the device with its capped, protruding lens and crank lever.

Alice unlatches each compartment at the back in turn and

shows Mr. Tanner the cunning brass workings. "See, I load the film on this bobbin—" She takes a fresh roll out of its box.

"Shouldn't this be done in the dark?"

"Don't worry, that problem's been solved—there's a black paper trailer at each end to shield it from daylight. Then this other spool here will take up the film—"

"Does that"—Mr. Tanner fumbles for the word in French—"is that what moves it along?"

"This crank, exactly, at top speed—the movement is like an eggbeater." But that sounds too housewifely; Alice wishes she'd found another way of putting it. "It takes over a dozen photographs per second."

"How marvellous."

She doesn't want to push too hard for a sale this early in the journey, and after all, the American can't be so very flush if he's travelling in Second like them. So she finishes preparing Demenÿ's camera for use—"Voilà"—then fastens all the compartments again.

As she sets the case down at her feet, she remembers why she brought up moving pictures in the first place. "When your improved model is ready to go on the market, Monsieur Gaumont, don't you think making our own demonstration films for illustrative purposes might help us sell more?"

Her boss makes a face at that. "We'd have to persuade people to sit in the dark and watch them."

"But we could furnish a comfortable little showroom at the office. If we offered something more interesting than the Lumières—"

"Each strip lasts only ten seconds," he reminds her. "Hardly time for anything very interesting."

"It should be possible to compose a sequence from several strips," Alice suggests. "Dozens of strips!"

"A sequence of what?" Gaumont looks at least mildly intrigued now, or maybe it's irritation. "The kind of souvenir a gentleman might try to capture at home—a meal, perhaps?"

Alice can't imagine anything more tedious than a film of a meal.

"Or a baby crawling in the garden?" he adds.

"I was thinking of something really captivating. Beautiful, even."

"A tree?" Gaumont suggests, quizzical. "But a tree doesn't move, of course, except in a high wind."

Mr. Tanner is shaking his head. "Beautiful? For that, we must turn to painting or sculpture."

Is he taking her boss's side against her?

Before Alice can find an answer, Gaumont asks him what he thought of the most recent Salon, and Mr. Tanner confesses that he showed three of his own canvases there, though, he acknowledges, to little acclaim.

And the conversation has wandered away and Alice has completely failed to explain what she wants, blast it. She puts her hand down and touches the camera's lid, which is vibrating along with the train.

10:44 a.m.
HALT FLERS

I don't know where you're fleeing to,
You don't know where I'm going,
You I could have loved,
And didn't you know it.

CHARLES BAUDELAIRE,
"TO A PASSERBY" (1860)

The moment the train comes to a stop, Marcelle de Heredia gathers her hat, coat, and bag. Her face is still hot; she's still cursing herself for having had the temerity to stick her nose in the Levassor family's business.

"Oh, is Flers your destination, mademoiselle?" Monsieur Bienvenüe is oblivious to the tension between the ladies.

Madame Sarazin-Levassor's silence is very loud.

Marcelle can't say yes in case they bump into each other again on the platform in Montparnasse. So she tells a smaller lie: "Ah, I noticed there's an empty carriage so I thought I'd get a little rest."

"Very good," Levassor says.

Everyone approves of women napping, Marcelle thinks crossly.

"*Figaro*, twenty-five centimes," a little girl pipes up from the platform.

Levassor fishes out a coin and leans out the window.

"There'll be a copy waiting on your desk at home, darling," his wife reminds him.

"But now's when I have the time to read it," he tells her.

With a stab of a hatpin through her hair, Marcelle's ready. She reaches for her typewriter.

"Need a hand with that?" Levassor half rises.

"No, no." Marcelle swings her Blickensderfer to prove its lightness and hurries down the carriage steps so fast, she almost turns her ankle.

Flers: Stumpy church towers, a covered market, what looks like a cotton mill, and a dye works spilling its stain into the river, which is the price of progress, she supposes. The platform's clogged with passengers getting off or on; some are just nipping out to buy a quiche or a bottle of cheap cider. Still hot-cheeked, Marcelle hurries along the train's length to find somewhere else to sit, almost colliding with a woman who can't be more than three feet tall, then having to steer around a man with an incongruously huge tank attached to his back. The next door is blue—Second Class—and Marcelle can see several heads in the window, so she keeps moving.

The camera salesman has been going on about the possibilities of colour photography, but Henry Tanner stopped listening when he noticed a young lady in navy blue pause on the platform outside and look up at his window almost as if she were trying to communicate with him. Tight black curls, dark eyes. She interests him somehow. He'd like to paint her, although he knows that models come in only two varieties: vain, wealthy ladies who hire painters and stone-broke girls whom painters hire. Her face is brown enough for her to have at least some African blood, like himself, unless that's wishful thinking. (Sometimes Henry lets himself dream of a kindred spirit who understands from experience the way he has to manoeuvre through an unpredictably hostile world.) Could that be one of the new portable typewriters she's carrying? Henry's summoning his nerve to bow to the intriguing young lady when she suddenly moves on.

"Don't you think Nadar's photographic portraits verge on art?" Gaumont asks now.

"Ah, possibly." *If only she'd chosen this carriage!* Henry could have gazed at her up close, exchanged a few remarks, even. He presses his cheekbone to the glass till it hurts. No sign of her; it's almost as if she was a figment of his imagination.

On impulse Henry stands, lowers the sash, and puts his head out. There's the back of her fishtailed blue skirt disappearing through the very next Second-Class door.

Funny how you feel the fatigue more when the train's standing still. But Guillaume can't really be tired yet, not after just over two hours of driving and only four into his ten-hour shift.

He opens the drain cocks at his feet to let the condensation run out, and the cylinders release a blast of steam. Two more minutes left here at Flers, or maybe only one ... frankly, once a trip's begun, he considers every moment his spirited engine isn't in motion to be a waste.

"I should oil those connecting rods." Victor's hoarse voice is loud in the quiet of the country station.

"Already?"

"She's been whining for a greasing this last quarter hour."

"Thirsty slut." Of course he and Victor wouldn't let anyone else speak of Engine 721 so.

"If she were to throw a rod ..."

Guillaume nods; that could pierce the side of the crankcase like a bayonet through a man's ribs.

His mate grabs the oil can and the grease jar and clambers around the side. For a man in his forties, Victor's quite the chimpanzee.

Here's a watery-eyed red-haired Cinderella standing below the footplate with her sack over her shoulder, shy of asking.

"For soapmaking?" Guillaume calls down.

"If you please, monsieur."

"Go on, then, help yourself."

The ash collector has her scoop out already and she reaches into Engine 721's ashpan eagerly.

Jean Le Goff appears beside her, waves a piece of paper at him.

Guillaume bends down to snatch it. Three neat words in a clerk's hand: *Halt at Briouze.* He sighs, a punctured balloon.

Victor's wooden clogs clang on the footplate. "Françoise dumping you at last, is she? Can't stand the smell of those feet for one more night?"

Guillaume breaks it to him: "They've added Briouze. That's our chance of making four o'clock out the window."

Victor groans. "Who the hell could need to board at Briouze? Not a soul lives there."

Guillaume tries to summon some humour. "HQ must be *trying* to make us late."

Victor nods vehemently. "It's a game to them. Or to whatever moneyed *connard* telegraphed to demand we make a special stop today. And since he must have his own coach-and-four to get him as far as Briouze, why couldn't he drive another, what, eighteen measly kilometres and board here at Flers with the rest of humanity?"

Guillaume shrugs, which sets something in his right shoulder twinging. He blasts the steam whistle, meaning *Can we bloody well get going?*

━━━

"Second Class, blue, at the back." Jean Le Goff's hands direct the human traffic as if he's the ringmaster in a circus.

107

Two new passengers have just been sprung from the fenced-off Second-Class waiting area under a huge poster offering trips to Mont Saint-Michel. Sportsmen, he'd guess, from their marsh waders and binoculars, though no guns, so the peculiar modern breed who bag the birds only in a manner of speaking, by recording them in their notebooks.

Jean charms and glad-hands, passes parcels and tosses cases; his pockets are getting heavy with coin already. A gent with two black eyes who smells of soap and fresh sweat asks permission, in an awful English accent, to put his bicycle in the baggage van.

Junior Guard Le Goff regrets to say that will cost one franc.

The Brit drops two like biscuit crumbs in his palm and urges him to be gentle with her.

"All aboard *now*," Mariette roars, hoarsely reproachful. The senior guard has been known to turn down tips on the grounds that they're for whores or beggars, a scruple that Jean finds comical.

Jean puts the bicycle into Rear Baggage with a show of care and directs the Anglo to squeeze into Front First.

"Anyone distinguished, is he?"

He turns his head to find that mannish girl with her metal lunch bucket. "Just a posh tourist."

She looks disappointed, like one of these fans who hang around stage doors. "Why's there no one in here?" she asks, jerking her thumb at Rear First.

Her curiosity tickles Jean. He counters with a question: "Something tasty in your bucket?"

She stares.

He angles a finger at her lunch. "Didn't dare leave it in Third while you stepped out in case they scoffed it?" She purses her lips. As she turns away, Jean murmurs: "We are making an extra stop at Briouze for a deputy for Orne, if that's *distinguished* enough for you?"

The young woman's not so plain when her face lights up with a grin from ear to ear.

Jean toots on his whistle. "Take your seats, mesdames, messieurs, the Paris Express is about to depart."

10:49 a.m.
DEPART FLERS

To save time is to lengthen life

REMINGTON TYPEWRITER
MOTTO (C. 1902)

Ticktock, how effortlessly, unrelentingly the minutes of this journey are clicking by. Engine 721 knows that the wheel of the earth always turns in the same direction, and time likewise. Human memory can spool it backwards, but that's just a magic trick.

A bird flies alongside, matching the train's speed. Will it blunder into her path and wind up smashed?

Engine 721 is not unfamiliar with death. The Company uses *accident on the tracks* to cover a variety of unfortunate incidents. If a blower gets blocked, flames may roar out of the firebox door, or sparks and cinders can set a field of stubble on fire. If a boiler's pressure climbs above seventy, it can burst. A wheel can overheat, a pump can clog, a connecting rod pop off, two carriages can uncouple without warning and jump apart.

To evade a guard inspecting tickets, panicking passengers have been known to open doors and fling themselves into ditches; not all of them survive to stumble to their feet. At a crossing, a curious child or tired labourer is unable to move fast enough to escape a glancing blow from a carriage's armoured side. A drunk conks out between two of the wooden sleepers that prop up the rails, and an oncoming engine erases him.

Such deaths of civilians are rare and always reported, whereas those of railway workers happen ten times as often but are hardly ever mentioned in the press. There is a silent consensus among the six companies that occasional man-glings on the job are to be expected. Surgeons are kept on re-tainer, to come quickly with their rolls of knives. Railwaymen have been snared between carriages during the shunting and been decapitated, cut in two, or burst like tomatoes.

Many years ago, circumstances obliged Engine 721 to halt in a tunnel for ten minutes, and her pent-up fumes asphyxi-ated the driver and stoker waiting on her footplate. She never meant them any harm; this is simply how she was made.

―――――

In Front Third, Mado seeps on. The rags in her drawers must be soaked half through now. She's too exhilarated to care. From what the guard said, it seems her plan to snare a mem-ber of parliament has worked.

A tiny, plump woman in a straw hat with hair so blond

it's almost transparent squeezed in beside her back at Flers. It's so crowded in here, Mado has her lunch bucket clamped between her boots on the floor to make sure no sway of the train or clumsy movement by a fellow passenger knocks it over before she's ready. Briouze is the next stop, and Briouze is when the deputy for Orne gets on and this train becomes (in a world where a hundred working folk are valued less highly than one of their *betters*) a prime target. Think how the government—all the governments of the world—will quake if Mado manages to kill one of their own!

Her stomach makes a long, loud growl.

The blonde half laughs. "Looks heavy." She nods at Mado's lunch bucket to show what she means. "Bet you like your grub."

You're fat is what she means, and she should talk. Mado gives her a stare.

The man with the bowler hat asks: "Not eating yet?"

"It's not even eleven," Mado replies without looking at him.

"Always famished hours before noon myself."

"It'll taste better later," she mutters.

The Russian—Blonska, that's the name—quotes drily, *"There's no sauce like hunger."*

The blonde swallows uncomfortably. "I'm so bedevilled by heartburn, I don't dare have a bite."

"Due soon, are you?" That's Blonska.

The blonde's eyes drop—she's a little embarrassed—and she nods.

Ah, not just plump but pregnant. Mado should have spotted that, but in her mother's case, it was always quite clear—the ball of flesh stood out from the skin-and-bones frame. She catches herself checking the woman's left hand, which does indeed have a thin band of gold. These leftover conventional judgements are hard to shed. *It doesn't matter now*, Mado reminds herself. *None of these people matter as individuals, including me.*

In a low voice, Blonska—who sounds like some kind of charity worker?—is drawing out the blonde. Madame Langlois, takes in sewing and ironing, constant heartburn since the summer . . .

Mado wishes she could shut her ears. She only has to sit tight till Briouze. *All of us in this carriage, maybe all of us on this train, our stories end today.*

<hr />

Second Class is a little shabby, Marcelle de Heredia is finding, and only part of the back divider is padded, but what does decor matter? Just five hours to go till Paris, and having even a shabby carriage all to herself is luxury.

Forget the Levassors, Marcelle orders herself. *That poor sick girl. And the mother had every reason to lose her temper with me.* Marcelle is better at the certainties of science than the ambiguities of social intercourse.

The Express is running alongside a stream now. There's a skinny fellow with rolled-up trousers crouching at the edge—frog-catching, maybe? And two red-armed laundresses farther along, twisting a bedcover to wring it out, sheets already spread on bushes.

To work. Marcelle lifts her machine out of its wooden casket and places it onto the tiny table. She adds a fresh ink roll and feeds in a sheet of paper. Only concentrated effort on her studies will be able wipe the whole mortifying conversation with Madame Sarazin-Levassor from her mind. She turns up the half-lamp overhead, but the oil smells, and the feeble light has a slight flicker to it, so she decides she's better off relying on daylight and turns it down again. She sits very upright on the uncomfortable bench and starts rat-a-tat-tatting loudly enough to put off anyone who might glance into the carriage at the next stop and think of joining her.

She's typing out her handwritten notes from a week ago and getting them in better order as she goes. This is an important study; she's helping her doctoral supervisor analyse the rate of nerve response in different types of muscle. How Marcelle loves her Blickensderfer's carapace, each letter hoisted on its little white pedestal in the familiar sequence— WZYB HFXK. Also the way this model lets you see what you've just written. She works the muscles of her fingers; her oval nails tap out a staccato tune. If she types fast enough, immerses herself deeply enough, she won't feel the time passing any more than a fish feels the water.

On this third leg of the journey, Léon Mariette rides in the Post Van, which smells of Camembert. As a Norman, he should be proud of the cheese—it's this very train line that has allowed the great white wheels in wicker baskets to cross the globe in weeks and win enduring fame—but sometimes the sweaty whiff is too much for him.

He checks each box and package against its papers to make sure it's been correctly identified, weighed, ticketed, and registered. You never know what people will try to send by parcel post: snakes, parrots, pickaxes . . . Even if a parcel has its origin station and destination written legibly on the correct colour card, labels can come ungummed and peel off or get stuck to other items and transfer themselves like ticks in long grass. Léon's world is one of bothersome objects: goods lost, delayed, in bad order, undercharges, overcharges. *Natural vice* covers the inherent tendency of barrel hoops to rust and soft fruits to go mouldy, say, which can't be considered the Company's fault, not to be confused with *negligence* (clumsy handling or violent shunting), which can result in tins dented or jars cracked and for which the Company and Senior Guard Mariette in particular may be held liable.

He reads a circular about a valuable bundle of fabrics that failed to turn up at Granville yesterday and writes out orders to the staff of each of this route's four stops to look for it. Even large, cumbersome objects can be found in dark corners if sought with sufficient zeal. Not that railwaymen are known for that trait. In Léon's view, the Company hires too many barely qualified brothers, sons, and nephews, and the union is protective of even its most undeserving members. When Léon catches a railwayman standing around smoking, he always quotes "Procrastination is the thief of time."

Harm can be done to parcels, but greater harm can come

from them; any one of these could be death delivered a box. Baggage doesn't make Léon nearly as nervous, because each owner travels on the same train as his own valise, and who'd blow himself up? But packages can be set by clockwork to go off at a precise moment days after the senders have made their getaway. Paris is said to have two thousand revolutionaries now, groups called the Starving and Hatred and Revolver in Hand, each with its own paper, cabaret, and soup kitchen. Some newspapers now run a dedicated column headed, with facetious brevity, *Dynamite.*

Last month Léon found a large hamper that smelled like boiled eggs and rattled oddly. Being unwilling to risk the lives of the train's passengers, he tossed it out the window into some bulrushes. Its owner never complained to HQ that it hadn't turned up, which went some way towards confirming Léon's suspicions.

He lets out an almighty yawn and knuckles his lower back. His made-to-measure corset helps the aching only somewhat. Léon hasn't been sleeping well. In recent dreams he's been struggling through bewildering paperwork, and on waking in the middle of the night, he lies there for hours in the dark.

Forty-two. Until this year, crews could cash out at fifty and still get a third of their salary every year for as long as they lasted. But now that some people are living so long, the Company's told the union it needs to squeeze more service out of each man on the books, so no one's allowed go till the age of fifty-five. Which means Léon has at least another thirteen years of intermittent backache before he can take his pension. Out in suburban Malakoff, Marie's already talking to the neighbours about that golden era *when my husband retires*, though how she intends to stretch a third of his pay to cover all their needs is far from clear. Anyway, Léon fears he wouldn't know himself without his job—like a goat used to the tug of his tether.

He checks the next parcel. Tedious work, but as he always says, *Safety takes no holidays.*

⊢────────┤

One Train Can Hide Another. This baffling line has become stuck in Maurice Marland's head. He thinks of a crowd of grown-ups, each one blocking the one behind from view. Are the thoughts in his mind like that too? Do the things he knows cover up the ones he doesn't?

He's reading *Around the World in Eighty Days*—which starts at a train station with the funny name of Charing Cross—but he's distracted by a man in the corner whistling a tune that Maurice nearly recognises. The sound is shrill, but nobody objects; passengers seem to pretty much make themselves at home here in Rear Third. The nurse is complaining to anyone who'll listen about the noise and stink of the railways. Monsters, she calls the great engines, insisting that she'd have delivered her charge back to Paris by stagecoach if her town still had one.

Maurice cranes his head over his shoulder to look at the tiny dolled-up girl, the package the nurse must hand over now. His eyes prickle. To think she's known only one home for four or five years and one (hired) mother, and now she's going to be deposited with the strangers who are her parents. Maurice never thought to be grateful that Maman and Papa weren't well-off enough to foster him out. Will the child ever see her nurse again? he wonders.

"A great big octopus, with tentacles going in all directions."

Maurice blinks. Where?

"It sucks up the young," the nurse rants on. "They come back to visit in fancy boots just to tell us we're *behind the times*."

"Don't know about that," the brick-brown labourer woman objects. "Young folk can stay home these days, send lace and butter off to market by train. Half these towns have only survived thanks to the railway."

The nurse clears her throat furiously. "But what about the quiet places that aren't on the line? They're dying all the faster."

In the rectangle of the window, Maurice sees a distant bridge flash like a knife.

He remembers a diagram his teacher drew on the blackboard of how the earth is always spinning like a top. How strange to think that this train and all who ride in her are dashing along eastwards, and so is the ground under her wheels—so does that mean they're really going twice as fast?

11:10 a.m. [unscheduled]
HALT BRIOUZE

*We anticipate the future as if it were too slow in coming,
as if to hurry it up, or we recall the past as if to halt its
rapid flight. We are so foolish that we wander in times
that are not ours, without thinking of the only one that is.*

BLAISE PASCAL,
PENSÉES (1670)

As they pull into Briouze, reversing steam to slow down,
Victor Garnier grasps the situation at a glance. On a
siding waits a lone train carriage with fresh varnish and curli-
cues and station staff flapping about; a local engine must
have hauled it this far. So the Express's unscheduled stop was
arranged at the last minute not to pick up some rich passenger but to allow him to hitch on. "Private carriage," Victor
calls to his driver as the train's noise lulls.

Guillaume shakes his head, incredulous, as they glide to
a standstill.

"Speed up again?" Victor suggests, poker-faced. "Leave him in our dust?"

Guillaume grins. "You would, wouldn't you? And that's why they'll never let you be a driver."

The real reason Victor won't apply for a promotion is that then he'd no longer be Guillaume's stoker. As a driver, he'd only glimpse Guillaume now and then in large stations with parallel tracks.

He cranes his neck to look at the glossy carriage, a fancy toy. "Why can't his nibs just plonk his arse down on sprung velvet?"

Guillaume snorts. "Thinks his farts don't smell."

The two rollers spend every second night in their room across from Granville Station, cots butted up against each other as snug as engine and tender. They sleep in the fug of each other's feet, so Victor can't tell Guillaume's smells from his own anymore. This is Company policy, to keep driver and stoker closer than brothers, because both speed and safety depend on the two knowing each other like catcher and flier on trapezes.

All along the convoy, people's heads are popping out like moles. Passengers jump out, and a dozen or so go around the back of the rudimentary station to relieve themselves. (The women will find they're out of luck.)

There's the senior guard grousing with the Briouze men halfway down the platform. Guillaume leans past Victor and shouts, "Time's a-wasting, Mariette. We'll shunt forward, you hook it on our tail."

Mariette calls back, "No, we're uncoupling halfway along so Monsieur Christophle's car can be with First Class."

Victor protests, "Even if it makes twice the work for us?"

"Wants to be warm and safe in the middle, like the youngest brother on a winter night," Guillaume mutters, staring at his watch as if his goggled eyes could somehow hold back the minute hand.

This Christophle must have given the stationmaster a fat tip, and the crew won't see a sou of it.

Victor takes his shovel and scoops some black fragments off the footplate to occupy himself. Running calculations, as ever. The hunger of Engine 721's furnace depends on the tonnage she's pulling but also on the slope. If Victor doesn't anticipate each upgrade on the route and boost the flames before his mate requires that surge of puff, she'll mount sluggishly or even stall (imagine the shame!). And if Victor's caught off guard by the next downgrade, when she'll start freewheeling, the pressure will be too high, and he'll have to vent expensive steam so it won't build up and burst the boiler, either scalding the two rollers or blowing them to smithereens.

He does what he can with the coal the Company sends him, dampening it from his water bucket to keep down the dust and prevent it from caking. He cracks or slices the lumps so the pieces will burn at an even rate. But the hard mathematics of his job means that it costs a kilo of coal to turn six litres of water to steam, and more coal than that if there are impurities. The railways have covered France so fast, and every decade the new trains are heavier and longer and move faster, so French coal's in chronically short supply, and much of it is dirty—yet if Victor and Guillaume use up the 721's whole allowance of the stuff, the Company cuts down their blasted bonus to nothing. It's only October; in the cold months it takes more fuel to feed a fire, so their forty percent shrinks away fast.

Restless, Victor jokes to try to lift his driver's mood: "Maybe the bigwig's a leper, can't bear to be seen by fellow passengers."

"Or horribly scarred," Guillaume contributes.

"The Man in the Iron Mask!"

Léon Mariette suddenly appears on the step below, his boots still shiny; does he polish them between stations? "By the way, Pellerin, it's no business of yours to tell me how to lay out the components of my train."

The two rollers cackle. "*Your* train?" Victor asks.

"You're in charge of the engine, but my responsibility covers everything and everyone on the—"

"You're just the passengers' nursemaid," Guillaume tells him.

It's an old argument; they're all just killing time.

A whistle from behind prompts Victor to lean out. "Unhooked," he reports to his mate. "Stationmaster's waving us forward to make some room."

Guillaume applies a little steam to nudge the front half on.

Like a chopped worm, Victor thinks. (He was the kind of kid who had to satisfy his curiosity about such things.)

As the station crew tow this Monsieur Christophle's carriage off the siding and fit it between the two sections of the train, more minutes crawl by. Victor feels the crew's Christmas pay for punctuality shrinking like an itch in his veins.

The pressure gauge needle's tilting over to the right. *Merde*; she needs venting. Victor opens the exhaust pipe and lets out a white jet, which forms a cloud around the engine. Watching the expensive steam dissipate, he rolls a cigarette. Crews aren't allowed to smoke on duty (or drink, or swear), but who'll see them up here? And it's not as if they're wasting time; time's a-wasting in spite of them, more like. He lights up, takes two pulls, then passes it to Guillaume. "That big carthorse"—gesturing towards a passing wagon—"would it derail us, do you think?"

Guillaume nods. "Without a doubt, size-wise."

"But would it be stupid enough to stand on the crossing with an express barrelling down? A sheep might be."

"We'd flick a sheep off the tracks, though," Guillaume points out.

"Half a dozen sheep in a huddle?"

Guillaume's scowling over his watch again. "Nearly six minutes behind already."

Although by any measure Albert Silas Christophle is an important man, the private carriage is for his wife.

"Is it done yet?" Anna, supine on her daybed.

"Almost." Albert has no idea; how can it be taking the sooty-faced fellows so long to attach a hook? But almost forty years of marriage have taught him the art of vague reassurance.

He had the carriage made with double doors to allow Anna's bath chair to be carried in at the start of each journey. Her bed's suspended from the roof to minimise jarring and draped in curtains on three sides to block draughts. The carpet is thick; three centimetres of felt underlay give it a mushroomy feel. Anna has a commode and a sink and a Chinese screen for privacy, handy on today's journey to keep little André from bothering his grandmother. The five-year-old, tucked between the screen and the window, is whispering to his felt elephant in a tailcoat. Adjustable blinds of gold tapestry exclude all but a fraction of daylight. André's game involves tapping on the tiny strip of bared glass but quietly enough that his grandfather hasn't had to scold him.

Albert stares out at the green field—the lush grass of Normandy on which its famous breeds of horses and cattle graze. It reminds him of a legend of a lord who happened across the hot spring at Bagnoles as he was leading his faithful steed into the forest to let him loose to crop grass for his remaining days. The knackered old stallion leapt into a steaming gorge and came out as lively as a colt. The lord dared to do the same and was transformed into a young man again. How wonderful if the deputy for Orne and governor of the Crédit Foncier bank could find some magical source of renewal and turn his own clock back . . .

Or Anna's. Turn it back even one year, to when she was sixty, lively, and happy—or happy enough. Before biliousness, fatigue, fainting spells, aches, and miscellaneous misery. (The doctors can't agree on a diagnosis let alone a treatment.)

Her skirt stirs, writhes, revolves; it's the little greyhound. Albert's wife always seems to wear shadowy hues these days, to match her pet. "Mignonette, stand up!" On the quilt, the dog gets up on her back legs in her travelling cloak, silver collar, and rubber boots. "Very good," cries Anna faintly. "Walk for me?" The dog manages to lurch around on two paws. "*Brava!*" A tight embrace, kisses.

These circus tricks make Albert sick. The creature was bred to race, and this is how she must spend her days? Another thing: Mignonette is so entirely silent that he wonders if the breeder could have cut her vocal cords.

"A train came in through the fireplace," his wife remarks.

Albert sometimes wonders whether the problem is not Anna's body but her mind. "What's that, *ma chère?*"

"In my dream, last night, the one I told you I couldn't remember."

Sometimes when she rabbits on, he keeps reading the paper and pays no attention. "A train ..."

"There was a fire in the grate, but the smoke turned to steam, and it was a train puffing towards me in the air!"

"A very little train?"

"You're doing it again." Anna takes off the blue glasses that shield her eyes. "Interrogating me in your mocking, lawyerly way."

127

Albert was already a lawyer when she married him, and now he's a bank governor and a politician too, and will she ever be satisfied? "I'm just trying to picture your dream."

"I expect I'll be prostrated for three days after this journey." And how will that be different from her usual state?

Limply Anna holds up her book. "This doctor says neurasthenia is a . . . what's the term? A *side effect* of rapid locomotion and instantaneous communications. Modern life is more than our hurried, harried nerves can bear."

Speak for yourself. Albert's nerves like locomotion, the more rapid the better. And if Anna believes high-speed transit is so noxious, why has she put him to the trouble and expense of this custom-made carriage?

Her sullen suspicion of the railways dates from before her mysterious illness. The Christophles were taking the train back from Vienna, and an obdurate guard who refused to speak any French wouldn't let the greyhound travel with them and insisted on tying her up in the baggage van. Anna was convinced that her poor Mignonette must have been subjected to the advances of some dog of a common breed that night and she had her repeatedly flushed out with vinegar as soon as they got back to Paris as well as treated prophylactically against fleas and mange. She believes a mésalliance can contaminate a bitch's litters for the rest of her life despite Albert's attempts to reason this superstition away.

"Attention!" Anna balances a sugar lump on her pet's nose. (She must have a supply of them among the bedding, which strikes him as unhygienic.) "Wait . . . wait . . ."

"May I have a lump?" André's oddly large head has come around the Chinese screen.

Anna doesn't look up. "They're for Mignonette, who's in training."

Albert's tempted to ask, *Wasn't it you who longed for grandchildren?*

"Training for what? For racing? She's not a racing dog, is she?"

"Obedience training." Albert gives his grandson a meaningful look.

"I can do training, too, for sugar, Grand-maman. Grand-maman!"

"Keep your voice down," Albert whispers.

But his wife, clutching her temples, is leaning back on the pillows.

Albert was rather hoping Jules-Félix and Emma Gévelot would offer to take André into First Class with them and keep him entertained. In his experience, the childless can go either way—dote on youngsters or shy away from them. Also, Albert's guests may be a little miffed at having to take a hired carriage from the Christophles' lodge to Briouze Station with their friend what's-her-name and not being invited to share these private quarters on the train. But really, letting six people crowd in here would defeat the whole purpose of an invalid carriage.

Albert and his fellow deputy for Orne have spent the past week at the lodge in Gué aux Biches to get in a bit of hunting. Anna not being up for playing the hostess these days, Emma

Gévelot and her friend—or paid companion; Albert still can't quite tell—had to amuse themselves. Meanwhile, the men bagged a wild boar and two roebucks between them; next time, Albert might propose duck flighting on the marshes. *Oh, come on, when will this so-called Express get going?*

Jules-Félix Gévelot tipped the moustachioed guard three francs to unlock the Rear First carriage for them. As the factory owner steps in, out of the corner of his eye he sees someone in the far corner—a disagreeable-looking old character with pouched eyes and an untidy beard. But when he, Emma, and Aimée settle into their seats, he realises with rueful amusement that it was his own reflection.

The decor of the car is opulent but it's not that large, so Jules-Félix is glad he sent their maid and manservant down to Third. "Christophle's royal litter seems to be taking an age to attach."

"Don't be peevish," Emma tells her husband, propping up her feet on the travel stool he brought along for her. The ladies have to face in the direction of travel because Aimée has a weak stomach. (Both the Gévelots call Emma's friend by her first name at her request, though the informality still makes him wince.)

"Did I sound peevish?" Jules-Félix likes Christophle perfectly well—he is a sound progressive and not too boastful a hunting companion.

"My dear husband is often rather crotchety on a train due to nerves," Emma remarks to Aimée.

He lets out a snort, which sounds huffy, he realises, although it's hard not to after such an accusation.

"Nervous of railway travel? How silly, and you're not even seventy," Aimée scolds him.

Twenty years older than the ladies. Jules-Félix bristles. "What has my age to do with it?"

"She means you've ridden on trains since you were a boy, so you should be used to them by now," Emma murmurs. "Your parents might have been worried that their eyes would cross or their brains would be bruised, but you know better."

"I'm not nervous of riding on a train," Jules-Félix snaps. A perverse honesty nudges him to add, "Though I can't say I like the idea of dying prematurely in one."

"Come now, what are the odds?" That's Aimée.

He picks one example. "There was a bridge in Scotland recently brought down by high winds that took a train into the river, and seventy-five souls with it."

"That would seem to prove the danger of bridges rather than trains, no?" Emma asks gravely. "Once home, we must resolve never to cross the Seine again."

His wife's gentle mockery manages to make Jules-Félix chuckle. "Mind you, avoiding bridges in Paris would be a splendid excuse to get us out of some tedious dinners."

She puts a hand on his knee. "You needn't rush into the Assembly this afternoon, *mon cher?*"

Jules-Félix shakes his head. The session opening's just a formality. "I'm saving my powder for Thursday, when the government's expecting a challenge over the glassmakers' strike."

"Oh, is that still dragging on?"

"The outlook's very bad," he tells her. "Extremist troublemakers everywhere—and, it must be said, tyrants putting them down. The police have started arresting the glassmakers' organizers and bringing in trainloads of scabs from all over France."

"I don't suppose you allow unionizing at your factory?"

Jules-Félix is wary of talking politics with his wife's friend, who thinks an arch tone makes up for her ignorance. "Ah, it hasn't arisen. We treat our workers royally—houses with gardens, a shelter for the aged, a nursery where mothers can feed their infants for an hour a day . . ." Most of the thousand-strong Gévelot workforce are female; those meticulous little hands are best for filling cartridges. "And we haven't had a fatality in twelve years." He doesn't mention the appalling sums his father had to pay the injured and the widowed in the early days.

"They never threaten a strike, then?" Aimée's really pressing him.

He shakes his head. "If they demanded a raise and cut the firm's profit margin, they'd risk putting us out of business— they would only be shooting themselves in the foot."

"With a Gévelot bullet, as it were!"

He grants her a half-smile.

Emma's already immersed in her book, some yellow-jacketed railway novel, probably sensationalist stuff. Of course, it's hard to concentrate on anything serious when you're on the move. The volume Jules-Félix picked up at the Hachette stall when coming down from Paris the other day isn't much better—a silly story about a machine on which a man can journey through time.

Though that would be worth the discomforts of the trip—time travel! Would Jules-Félix choose to go forwards, out of curiosity? Or backwards, maybe to when he was eighteen, just before his father died and he had to help his mother run the munitions works? The new responsibility was an honour, yes; he inherited a great name and has made it greater. But it was an abrupt departure from boyhood, and the half a century since has passed in a blink.

Not for the first time, Henry's sunk in self-reproach. That dark young lady—the one who's preoccupied him since he spotted her getting into the next carriage at Flers—is at this very moment sitting perhaps a metre away behind a thin wall. As long as the train is held up here at Briouze, what's preventing him from moving to hers and striking up a conversation? Nothing at all—if only Henry had the spunk.

He goes back to brooding about his work, his *Lazarus*, in particular. In the biblical account, the practical sister mentions that it's been four days, and her brother is beginning to stink. But then Jesus calls, *Lazarus, come forth*, and out of his tomb the man walks, shaking off his wrappings. Lazarus the puzzle, the freak, the glory. Henry has difficulty believing literally in the miracle—that the stink turned back to sweet as the cells obeyed the divine command to function again, that Jesus reversed those four days.

A guard's whistle. The stampede of passengers leaping back in.

The sound galvanises Henry and he finds himself on his feet—"Aha, I believe I see someone I know"—snatching his things from the net. Mademoiselle Guy looks up, puzzled, from *The Human Beast* as he nods to her and to her boss—Gaumont, was it?

He scrambles out and down and takes five strides along the platform to the steps of the other Second-Class carriage. The whistle sounds again, so he yanks open the door and practically throws himself in.

The young lady's alone, he's glad to see, and working at her typewriter—or, rather, frozen over the keys, staring at him. Henry's muscled in, forcing a tête-à-tête. He musters his French: "Terribly sorry, mademoiselle. My carriage was very crowded."

"That's quite all right." Her voice is sweet, but it's clear that she wanted to be alone.

Henry fits his limbs into the corner diagonally across from her. What kind of thug is he to have barged in here and trapped her in this tin can with him for the next hour? This is the kind of behaviour that gives Americans a bad name.

The young lady starts to type again, with remarkable speed. Henry shuts his eyes and leans his head back, trying to absent himself and let the atmosphere seal up the rip he's torn in it.

Mado lets down the window with a thump, sticks out her head, and cranes her neck to see past Rear First to where the new carriage has been hitched on. Her lunch bucket is held steady on the floor, clamped between her boots. She just needs to be quite sure that the one for whom the train's made the special stop is on board.

"Monsieur," she calls to the train guard, the younger one with the moustache, "he's in that fancy carriage, is he?"

"Only one of them is."

She stares, confused.

The guard points to the private carriage and then the green door of Rear First beside it. "It just so happens we're honoured by the presence of *two* parliamentary members for Orne Department today."

Mado's heart leaps painfully in her chest. A pair of those bastards, and so close to where she's sitting. This is a sign: the right day, the right train, and she's the right one to do it.

Now, she tells herself. She should flip her device upside down this minute, while she's powered by thrilled conviction. It's the work of a moment. She reaches down. grasps the smooth cylindrical sides, picks it up, and sets it on her lap. *Ready, Mado? Ready at long last?*

The guard says something that's drowned out by the engine's steam whistle.

"What's that?" she calls.

"And would you believe, mademoiselle, a third will be getting on at Surdon!"

Mado goggles at him.

A handbell rings farther up the platform. The guard blows the final whistle before climbing into Middle Third with a call of "Tickets, please," and the train starts to move.

Very carefully, Mado sets her lunch bucket back down on the floor.

DEPART BRIOUZE

Watch the curves, the fills, and tunnels,
Never falter, never quail,
Keep your hand upon the throttle,
And your eye upon the rail.

MASON ELLIS ABBEY,
"LIFE'S RAILWAY TO HEAVEN" (1890)

O n we go.

This is not the first time Engine 721 has encountered one of those rare humans who are careless of their own lives or even positively eager to throw them away.

The jumpers, the crews call them, since that's usually how they do it. Every year a few—generally men, the sex more given to violent methods—make use of the massive momentum of a train. They stand waiting rather too near the track as if merely curious but with the hectic eyes of lovers. At the last moment they dash madly—or walk calmly—under the wheels and force the train to paint the shining rails with their blood.

It's an awful trick to play on the rollers standing on the footplate. Sometimes a jumper will even look the driver or stoker in the eye when stepping forward, as if to put it on him.

After each such incident, the Company has the engine hosed down and polished, then sends it back out, gleaming, the next morning because the circulation must not, cannot, stop or the whole system could seize up. Newspapers sometimes blame the railways for the rising rate of self-murder, but a train never commands or lures a man to throw himself down. In every age, ways have been devised to unseal a bag of skin, and if not by train, a determined person will find another means.

So Engine 721 has been involved in suicides, yes. But today is her first bomb.

Such a makeshift, primitive apparatus Mado Pelletier's lunch bucket holds in contrast to this train's vast and exquisite mechanics—yet potentially just as powerful. Death on a grand scale, carried like a terrible secret inside the Express today.

And Engine 721 can do nothing to stop it. She's not indifferent to the prospect of annihilation. She'd spare her frail passengers terror and pain if she could. But she has no means of saving them any more than she does of saving herself.

The American painter, oddly, rushed out of the carriage, so when the Express rattles away from Briouze, Alice Guy and her boss are alone.

So awkward. She's remembering a Maupassant story about a cruel husband separated from his wife who happens to encounter her on a night train to the south. The twist is that the wife has engineered the meeting because she's become pregnant by her lover, and being seen disembarking with her husband at Nice is all she needs to pass the baby off as legitimate when it's born. As if carriage-sharing is a form of copulation!

Well, Alice might as well seize the opportunity she's been looking for. "Monsieur," she begins. Too rapidly, urgently; she wants this so much that she can't control her excitement.

Gaumont pulls at his moustache.

"There's a topic that's been on my mind for some time, one I've hesitated to broach, though you may have guessed it from hints I've dropped."

Uneasily: "I'm going to stop you there."

"No, no, please let me—"

"Really, mademoiselle, I'm a married man."

The groan bursts out of Alice, as loud as a horn.

Gaumont looks appalled. "My dear young lady."

Can he imagine this is the frustration of a spinster longing for his touch? Christ, the vanity of men. Or the vanity of Alice, for deluding herself that the men at work think of her as a colleague rather than a bit of skirt. Gaumont's out of his seat now, rearing up, looming, wobbling as the train rattles on. About to lurch towards her or away? Why, oh, why did Alice agree to accompany him on this wretched trip? This is going to end in mortification and Alice losing her job.

She tries a courteous voice with just a hint of steel. "Pardon, monsieur, you misunderstand me *entirely*."

He stares, blinks.

At such moments do men, like women, feel like actors handed scripts they have no time to read before being nudged onto the stage? "What I wanted to ask about is strictly a work matter."

"Business of the firm?"

"Quite so."

"Ah. Very good." His tone now flatter. Disappointment? Or possibly relief? It doesn't matter, because either way, Gaumont drops back down heavily onto the bench.

Alice presses on. "What I was saying earlier, about demonstration films."

He squints as if he doesn't recall. Then nods. "Yes, yes, I'll give that some thought when I have time."

But Paris is still more than four hours away. "While you're considering the question, perhaps I could borrow this camera of Demenÿ's?" Her fingers settle on its polished lid.

Gaumont tilts his head to one side. "To make one of these little films?"

No, to bake tarte tatin in, Alice almost snaps. "Yes, and more than one—half a dozen trial runs, perhaps. Entirely on my own time, you see, outside business hours." *But wouldn't*

I need daylight? At the weekend, then. "To show you and your partners the possibilities."

"What kind of possibilities?"

Alice fumbles for the right words: "Stories. But told only through pictures."

"Like ABC books for children? Or comics in the daily paper?" Gaumont's tone is verging on scorn.

"*So* much more gripping, though, monsieur, because these images would be moving. Performers acting, dancing, doing acrobatics, tricks." Alice remembers his banal suggestion of a baby crawling in a garden and tries to liven it up. "What about . . . a fairy plucking infants out of cabbages?"

Gaumont squints as if she's gone mad.

"It could be charming," Alice says weakly. "Hilarious."

"A man's not going to pay hundreds of francs for a piece of scientific equipment to look at fairies. At actors *pretending* to be fairies," he corrects himself in a withering tone.

The hypothetical customer's wife might persuade him, though, since that's how half the goods in Paris get sold—but this is an argument for another day. "Forget the fairy, then. It could be . . . soldiers duelling or revolutionaries storming a barricade."

"Too political."

"A ship in a storm?"

"How on earth would you—"

"I don't know! I don't know *yet*, I mean, but I'm sure it could be done." Alice improvises wildly. "A burglar sneaking through a house. A man jumping off a speeding train!"

141

"Why is he jumping off a speeding train?"

"Well, exactly, you're curious." She flails on. "Salome asking for the head of John the Baptist? A dog stealing sausages?"

The corner of Gaumont's mouth crinkles.

"Something to keep them watching our film to the last frame to see how it turns out."

He narrows his eyes. "You're very . . . passionate."

It sounds like a rebuke. Is he expecting an apology for her excess of enthusiasm?

"I'm not quite convinced, Mademoiselle Guy."

"Of course you're not—not yet," she murmurs. "Wait till you *see* what I can make." Should she dare bring up the fact that Gaumont began his career as a secretary himself? He might be offended by the comparison. She hints: "You must know that a secretary can have a good idea once in a while?"

A short laugh. "Even a stopped clock is right twice a day."

Gaumont's only teasing, which men love to do to pretty women. *He hasn't said no.* Alice smiles through set teeth.

As Blonska knits on, she's getting the full story out of the pregnant blonde, Cécile Langlois. She can't help herself; impossible to take a holiday from being concerned about people.

The problem turns out to be that the man who put that ring on her finger, Langlois, has been dead two years. The fellow responsible (as Blonska refers to him, though *irresponsible* might fit better) for the infant that's on its way is only twenty. He had no chance to marry Cécile before beginning his military service.

Blonska privately scoffs at that; a wedding takes ten minutes. "Will he acknowledge it, at least, so you can put his name on the birth certificate?"

Cécile swallows a sob and pushes tendrils of light gold off her face. "Too late—he's been sent off to Madagascar. I've been staying with my parents—keeping indoors so no one in town will know my state. I'm going to stay with my married sister in Paris, then bring the baby back with me and pretend it's hers and needs country air."

Blonska sighs at the complicated scheme, doubting the blonde's neighbours in Flers will be so easy to fool. She and Cécile are speaking low, out of discretion, but nobody else in Front Third seems to be paying much attention. Two are reading papers; one is chewing on a *saucisson sec*; one is refilling his pipe; and several have nodded off, as is common at this point in a train journey. The weary maid, Madame Baudin, has her head back and rolling as if her neck's been snapped.

"This is what's wrong with the world." The short-haired girl, Mado Pelletier, opens her eyes reluctantly.

"Beg your pardon, mademoiselle?" Cécile Langlois says.

Mado speaks as if the words are fighting their way out of her mouth. "Armies and governments and churches and bosses all keep men down, and men keep us down—our sex gets the worst of it."

She's oversimplifying, as the very young tend to do, but Blonska can't disagree. "I've never had any time for religion myself."

That surprises a smile out of Mado. "Yes! This fairy tale about the immortal soul—"

"People seem more like penny candles to me," Blonska says. "When the wax melts away, the flame's snuffed out."

"That's why I left school—those harping nuns."

Blonska demurs: "Education's useful, though."

The girl's lip curls. "I can educate myself."

Well, only to an extent. "*Knowledge is power.*" Was it Bacon who wrote that?

"But knowledge is not the only kind of power."

As Mado goes off on a long rant about oppressions of all varieties, Blonska nods along. The girl is indeed well-read—a testament to the free libraries provided by the state she so scorns, Blonska could point out if she were able to get a word in—and well-versed in the forces that have shaped her impoverished childhood.

The jargon's familiar to Blonska from her days in left-wing émigré circles, and so is the mood of electric resentment. When Blonska first grew tired of ladies in frills proposing teas and bazaars to raise funds, she used to go to soup-and-speeches evenings thronged with unemployed workers and radical artists. She liked to drink in the atmosphere of burning zeal flavoured with rage. One night she heard the old Communard Louise Michel, a grey-haired woman back from a decade of exile in the South Seas, speak of revolution as a flood tide, an avalanche, an earthquake that would turn the world upside down. It made sense, but only in the same way as a nocturne by Debussy made sense, in the language of pure, irrefutable emotion.

If Blonska weren't such a doubting Thomas, she might have been won over years ago. She's not proud of the cynicism that's kept her from joining any lost cause. She jumps in: "But we can't delude ourselves into thinking that tearing down this society will make a better one."

"It's not delusion. It's the only hope left," Mado counters.

"Come, now! Slogans and songs, marches and riots, never yet stopped a child crying."

The other women's discussion seems to be too abstract for Cécile Langlois, who's mopping her sweaty face and has undone two buttons to loosen the strings of her maternity stays.

Mado's now going on about the appalling unfairness of privilege being doled out according to the accident of birth.

"Unless there's no such thing," Blonska mutters.

That brings the young woman up short. "What?"

"*No accidents, only fate misnamed.* That's what Schiller said."

Mado's dry lips purse. "How defeatist."

"On the contrary, Schiller was known for his loud resistance to tyrants."

"But to take refuge in this mystical notion of destiny—"

"Is it mystical?" Blonska shrugs. "To me, it describes the way things work. A train can run only on the tracks laid down for it."

"So we're powerless to do anything about *the way things work?*"

"I didn't say that at all," Blonska says a little crisply. "Perhaps it's our *destiny* to try. The attempt to right wrongs is all the braver for its difficulty, no?"

"Its impossibility," Mado corrects her.

Blonska's been wrestling with this problem three times as long as this youngster. "Life is long," she tells her. "If you're lucky, that is."

Mado produces a hollow laugh at the word *lucky.*

Blonska searches her memory for an example. She drops her voice: "I recently met a journalist convinced that Captain Dreyfus is the victim of a conspiracy."

"Dreyfus the spy?" Mado asks, incredulous.

"Evidence was forged, he told me, anti-Semites gave false statements—" Blonska holds up her hand to forestall the girl's objections. "I can't say if there's anything to it myself. But when I pointed out to this fellow, Lazare, that clearing Dreyfus's name seemed a hopeless task, since the Jews always get the blame and magical reversals happen only in the theatre, what he said was *Blonska, justice is a long game.*"

"Not just long," Mado says hotly, "more like never-ending."

"Well." Blonska is a little impatient with the girl's impatience. (She recognises the irony in that.) "At least we can resolve to leave the dirty world a little cleaner than we found it."

"You're talking about charity?"

The scorn with which Mado pronounces the word! Blonska

quotes levelly, "*From each according to his ability,* and this is mine."

"You do-gooders are always coming around holding your noses, telling us to say our prayers, *wait for things to improve,* and, in the meantime, somehow *better ourselves!*"

"I've never made any such idiotic remark."

"Well. Even so. Charity just papers over the cracks. Oils the rustiest cogs of the machine."

The girl's not exactly wrong. "But ask a rusty cog if it would like to be oiled," Blonska urges. "Ask a hungry child if a loaf might be better than nothing."

Mado stares into space, her pupils like bottomless wells.

Mado Pelletier was that hungry child, Blonska thinks. Did no one ever offer her a loaf without a homily? "You grew up in Paris?" Guessing from the accent.

A nod. Then one detail: "In a greengrocery."

That surprises Blonska. "Lots of fruit, then?"

A snort. "Baskets full of pears and carrots and such but forbidden to us in the back room until they were overripe or wrinkled or mouldy. Once I punched an apple hoping I'd get to eat it when the bruise showed. But my mother somehow knew what I'd done and slapped my hands raw."

Blonska's face wrinkles with sympathy. "I suppose she was trying to teach you *the way things work.*"

Mado's jaw grinds. "There was no need for extra lessons. How things worked for her was, every year she'd be having another baby."

147

"So you have dozens of brothers and sisters?"

A violent shake of the head. "I'd be sent to fetch the midwife and make *preparations* . . ."

"Why you?"

"The only daughter." Mado pronounces the word with disgust. "I'd do whatever the midwife said—I was a *great help*. But every time, my mother would lose the baby."

"Oh, *ma chère*." Blonska almost whispers it.

———

In the Christophle carriage, Albert lets his eyes unfocus to blur the newspaper's fine print about the fiery speech expected from the socialist deputy for Tarn. He's so very bored.

Really, he chivvies himself, *you have no cause for complaint.*

The Christophles have come up fast. Albert's grandfather was a ploughman but made a lawyer of his son, and Albert himself wears the red rosette of the Legion of Honour on his lapel, and so does his own son Georges; see how the family line advances upwards across the page of history. A son and daughter grown, four grandchildren already. Albert and Anna have never lost a child either—she was healthy and vigorous right through her fifties.

This tedium is simply how it is to age alongside the woman he chose, the one who's now an invalid. Most likely she feels the same way about Albert, for all his vigour. He has no complaints, then, or no legitimate ones, only the restless gloom of a man of sixty-five. Only a yearning for something to happen that hasn't happened a million times before.

Framed briefly in the window, a castle like a chess piece discarded by giants. A minute later, a shrine—a miniature church, no wider than a metre, to house a statue of the Virgin, gaudy in blue and white. Albert's lip twists into an automatic sneer. Then he scolds himself for forgetting that many of those who elected him still hold to these soothing old beliefs.

The itch (as Albert calls his particular private craving) is bad today. Or *strong*—that might be a better word, because the desire doesn't pain or distress him; more like a dog pricking up its ears at sounds its owner can't hear. (But is Anna his dog owner in this analogy? Or is Albert's mind the hapless owner of his doggish body?) He's been in a slightly roused state all morning, perhaps because he's been released from the obligations of a host after the Gévelots' visit, but he's not yet back in the city. It's an in-between day, in transit; on a train, all one has to do is pass time.

So Albert lets himself consider certain spots on his mental map of the capital. Even the slimmest chance of an encounter this evening feels delicious, the friction of longing against possibility. He won't have enough time to go for a wander in his favourite wooded expanses of the Jardin du Luxembourg. But there are many smaller crannies to try, tucked away and out of the scrutiny of polite society. The *chalet de nécessité* with the gingerbread roof on Place de la Madeleine, for instance. The urinals off Les Halles have pierced patterns in the metal that let the sunshine through. The six-box one on Place de la Bourse with modesty screens that come down almost to the ankles. The very best—the eight-staller in the Champs-Élysées Garden encircled by a thick screen of evergreen bushes. Spots where no one's going to see this important bank governor cum politician. (Not that what two men get up to is a crime, technically, not since the revolution, but being caught with trousers down would risk a charge of public indecency, which would be a humiliating end to the glorious career of Albert Silas Christophle.) That two-booth steel pissoir outside the Santé Prison—Albert's had a quick and glorious suck-off there, and no passersby counted feet, or if they did, they didn't call the gendarmes. Generally the plain people of Paris are too busy earning their bread to give a hoot how others take their pleasure, which is one reason why it's the most civilized city on earth.

Albert enjoys this kind of slow anticipation so much that he almost prefers it to the blinding excitement of an actual coupling. If he had a choice between a whole day of thinking about it and two minutes of unexpectedly doing it, he'd probably choose the former. (Depending on the man, of course.) But the best is to have both: to want it all day, daydream about a grope or a suck, then get it . . . now, that would be bliss. That would fit him to take up the mantle of silver-whiskered statesman and family man once more.

"Albert!"

"I beg your pardon?"

"I asked you for a little water," says his wife faintly.

"Right away, *ma chère.*"

The carriage sways. Holding on to the table as he fills a glass from the jug, Albert finds himself wishing he had a bit of privacy to rub himself off. But for all the invalid carriage's luxurious fittings, there's no discreet corner out of view of woman and child. So he sits down and crosses his legs the other way.

Ever since he switched to the young lady's carriage at Briouze, Henry Tanner hasn't managed to say a word. *Craven chicken-heart*, he tells himself. *Gutless mouse. Spineless jellyfish.* If he fails to say so much as *Good day*, how will he ever know whether she's open to making his acquaintance? How can he ever expect to find a female friend, a companion to soften the rigours of this rootless artistic life? If not this lovely person with her air of calm intelligence, who is he waiting for?

A cluster of squat towers flashes by. A blue signboard: *Écouché-les-Vallées*. How beautiful French place-names are, even those of the ugliest towns.

Tap, tap; the deft pecking of a hungry bird. Whatever the dark young lady is typewriting, it seems marked by precision and purpose. Is that a name neatly inked on the side of the mechanism's case? Henry squints without moving his head. *De Heredia*—a Spanish name, perhaps?

Next up should be Argentan. Yes, here's the massive Plantagenet keep and then the slim spires of two Gothic churches, awfully paintable. Henry's spirits sometimes quail at the sheer number of his competitors, but most have clung to the coast, so there must remain some out-of-the-way inland spots that haven't been painted yet, surely?

Mademoiselle de Heredia, then. (Not *Madame*, Henry hopes; she doesn't look married, somehow, and wears no ring.) Maybe she's not of mixed origins at all, just Spanish or Italian or Greek. Also, he might have misread her manner when he let himself into her carriage back at Briouze; instead of politely resigned, she might be rigid with suspicion of the intruder. How little we know about the strangers we sit beside.

After another long stretch, it strikes Henry that the Express must be almost at Surdon, where other passengers might very well barge in just as he did. But still he can't seem to speak. He feels too much; he's cast his most feverish hopes on this quiet, intent person like a magic lantern show on a blank wall.

It's the silence that finally rouses him. Well, not silence—it's always noisy on a train—but the cessation of tapping. She fits her machine into its case, slides her papers into the compartment, snaps everything shut.

Apology unlocks his tongue at last. He pauses for a split second to translate his thoughts. "Parson me, mademoiselle, I've disturbed you."

"You haven't." She sounds perfectly Parisian. "I've finished."

Still Henry hesitates. He squeezes out some inoffensive remark about the loveliness of Normandy. He tries a follow-up: This is a region of France he could imagine making a home in.

She says her work is always likely to keep her in the capital.

To force an introduction, he ventures to ask about the name on her case.

Mademoiselle de Heredia says her father is Cuban in origin, though her mother, like her, is French-born.

Lots of African ancestry in Cuba; Henry catches himself grinning. He gestures at the typewriter. "You're a journalist, perhaps?"

She shakes her head. "I'm . . . well, the fact is"—she switches to excellent English—"I'm training to be a physiologist."

Can she tell from Henry's vacant look that he has no real idea what that is, even though she's speaking his native tongue as a kindness to him?

"I study living organisms," she explains, "their components, their interactions with their environments. Specifically their nerve responses."

His eyebrows go up. He hasn't met many scientists and never a lady one. "How, if I may ask, did you come to take up that . . ." *Business? Profession?* "Line of work?"

A little shrug. "I suppose it began with an interest in life in all its variety."

Life in all its variety; Henry likes the phrase.

"When I was very small, my father showed me a drop of water under a microscope magnified a thousand times."

"Was it so wonderful?"

"Horrifying," Mademoiselle de Heredia corrects him. "Paris water—the things swarming in every drop!"

That makes Henry chuckle. "Is he a scientist too?"

"A politician, retired now. He was once president of the municipal council."

Again, Henry knows his face must look blank.

"Like the mayor of your New York or Chicago?"

"Ah!" Remarkable; how did a Cuban of colour end up running Paris?

She seems to read his mind, and her face tightens. "Bigots used to call Papa 'the Chocolate Deputy.'"

Henry winces. This is the moment when he can match her candour, gift for gift: "American journalists sometimes dub me 'the Darkie Painter.'" Oh, but he omitted to tell her he was a painter in the first place.

"Ugh!"

With a single syllable, a childish expression of disgust, she's cleared the air. He smiles back at her, suddenly at ease. "Black newspapers call me *the hope of the race*, which I dislike for the opposite reason."

"The pressure to excel?"

She understands exactly. "Your father—I hope he persisted in the face of the scoffers?"

"Of course." Mademoiselle de Heredia makes a gesture as if to swat away a swarm of mosquitoes. "He's fought for votes for women, limits on the working day for children—"

"How marvellous."

"He always says, *Marcelle, don't let their foolishness get in the way of the work.*"

She's let slip her first name, or perhaps dropped it like a handkerchief for Henry to pick up: Marcelle. "My father is a bishop." But now Marcelle may be picturing someone very grand. "In the African Methodist Episcopal Church," he explains. "He was a barber before that. He tried to apprentice me in the flour trade."

"As a florist?"

She's heard him wrong, and he snorts at the misunderstanding. "No, wheat flour, milling. It made me wheeze."

Marcelle covers her musical laugh. "Your father hadn't noticed your artistic talent?"

Henry sighs. "He just didn't think it any way for a grown man to make a living."

"Ah. How shortsighted of him."

Well, that remains to be seen. "Last time I was home in the States, he grilled me about my sales in France—whether I'll ever earn enough to buy a house or support a wife." *You sound feeble, Henry. Woebegone. You've seized this chance to talk to a charming woman scientist, and all you can tell her is what a failure your daddy thinks you are?*

Henry feels a tugging, a pressure in his body, as the train slows. They're on a windswept plateau, a nowhere that a lone sign identifies as *Surdon*.

12:11 p.m.

HALT SURDON

*The ticking of the clocks sounds
like mice nibbling at time.*

**ALPHONSE ALLAIS,
THE BLACK CAT (1890)**

Jules-Félix Gévelot watches a score of passengers hop off with the constrained gait of people in urgent search of a latrine. (Where station facilities exist, they're so nasty, most men relieve themselves out the window as they're passing through the countryside. Emma and Aimée have already used a boat-shaped china *bourdalou* under their skirts, which Jules-Félix has emptied for them.)

Surdon seems nothing more than a hub for those changing trains on their way to or from Caen to the north or Le Mans to the south. An engine screams by and Emma jumps.

Aimée seizes her hand. "Darling, it's only the down train."

"Who's nervous now?" Jules-Félix can't resist the quip.

His wife ignores that. "Remember that night at the Gaieté, Aimée?"

"The theatre in Montparnasse?" He rarely has the time to take his wife to anything. "What happened?"

"It was nothing," Emma assures him. "Some scenery fell down with a clatter backstage, and half the audience bolted, screaming *Anarchists!*"

"We could have died in the stampede, thanks to those idiots," Aimée complains.

Or you could have been burnt alive if it really had been a bomb, Jules-Félix doesn't say. If people are jumpy these days, haven't they reason to be?

He thinks of poor President Carnot, gutted like a pig. And in the Chamber of Deputies, when that drifter tossed his nail bomb—Jules-Félix happened to be there that day. He remembers a boom and a fog, a clattering, screams. How random it seemed, whose flesh those flying nails found—for instance, three deputies from Morbihan who weren't even sitting together. The sixty or so who got hurt included some watchers in the gallery: a waiter, a tailor, a nurse ... Jules-Félix picked a nail out of a spatter browning on the floor and kept it as an aide-mémoire.

This latest president—Faure, an inoffensive leather merchant—is so desperate to make peace that he's declared amnesty for the anarchists, appealing for an end to governmental retaliations and guillotinings. That probably would be the best thing for France, but try persuading the crazies ...

Mouth against Aimée's ear, Emma says something that Jules-Félix doesn't catch; Aimée giggles.

On the whole he's glad his wife has her friend to keep her company. The fiction is that Aimée is merely visiting the Gévelots for long stretches, even coming with them on trips such as this latest one to Christophle's country place, but as far as he's aware, she has no other home.

No one could disagree that the Gévelot marriage has been a success. Emma's military connections were invaluable in helping the firm become such a pillar of the state that last year its official name was changed to the French Society of Munitions. At this point, Jules-Félix doesn't much care that the two of them no longer share a bed; almost two decades his junior, Emma must find him rather an old man, one who values unbroken sleep when he can get it.

There've been no children, though, which is rather a pity. Too busy to look for a bride, Jules-Félix was almost forty by the time they married, but still, many men sire offspring later than that. The matter's never been explained medically. Jules-Félix thinks of it as he would a lingering problem at the works. A cartridge without a bullet is termed a *blank*; a *dummy* is completely inert; a *dud* has powder but fails to ignite; and a *squib* ignites but without enough power to push the bullet out of the barrel. Whether Jules-Félix is a squib, dud, dummy, or blank is unclear, and he supposes it comes to the same in the end.

"My, my," he murmurs now, finger to the window glass.

On the platform, a gentleman with a monocle holds a case in each hand. He stands in close confabulation with a matron with glossy brown hair, a canary-yellow dress, and a basket.

"What is it?" Eager for entertainment, Emma and Aimée lean over to see.

"Here's another of my fellow deputies for Orne—the comte de Lévis-Mirepoix." Jules-Félix also knows the aristo from military circles; the Lévis-Mirepoix steam sawmill makes clogs for the same soldiers who are supplied with Gévelot bullets. But politically the two are poles apart. The comte recently had the gall to vote against free primary education.

"So that's the comtesse with him, in yellow?"

He chuckles. "No, *ma chère*. I happen to remember that his wife, mother of a half a dozen Lévis-Mirepoix—"

"Half a dozen?" Aimée sounds incredulous.

"Conservatives *and* Catholics," Emma murmurs.

"Is a blonde," he finishes.

His wife tilts her chin. "Is that so? Now, we mustn't leap to judgement. Could the comte have been recently widowed and remarried?"

Jules-Félix shakes his head. "I'd have heard. All those hours we stand around at the Assembly waiting for a vote to be called ... politicians are inveterate gossips."

"Some ladies of our age do colour their hair." That's Aimée, being ostentatiously fair.

"To cover up silver, yes," Emma concedes, "but from blond to brunette, really?"

He snorts. "No, this has to be a hole-in-the-corner affair." Lévis-Mirepoix's figure is remarkable for a man in midlife— wide shoulders, narrow waist—which he must owe to a superbly tailored corset. The brunette's face (not young, but pleasing) is familiar.

"It's the hypocrisy of the old snoot that bothers me," Emma tells her friend.

Jules-Félix, who must have twenty years on the comte, grins at *old snoot.* "Indeed. These pious monarchists are always harping on about *family* and how much more virtuous the nation was before the revolution." Since the whole snarling pack brought down Dreyfus last year, they've been insufferable; can't they get it into their heads that they don't run France anymore? He squints through the glass. "I'm almost certain . . . yes, *mon Dieu,* she's Riotteau's sister."

"Who's Riotteau?" asks Aimée.

"Riotteau the shipowner who represents Manche?" That's Emma.

He nods. "Used to be mayor of Granville, a good progressive."

Aimée protests: "So the lady in yellow's brother is yet *another* of your fellow deputies? This is like a gathering of a subcommittee."

"I suppose they're all heading back to Paris for the new session," says Emma.

Jules-Félix strains his memory. "Riotteau's sister been married for decades to a fellow of the name of Heureux. Or L'Heureux, maybe?"

"Love across the divide," Aimée croons, "a leftist's sister of a certain age and a royalist count criminally, fatally, drawn together!"

"And caught out at a railway station," Emma adds, "like something from a Feydeau farce."

As if the comte de Lévis-Mirepoix has somehow heard through the sooty glass, he catches his colleague's eye and blanches.

Jules-Félix smiles silkily and gestures for the pair to join them.

But the comte backs away from the brunette, muttering out of the corner of his mouth, and sets down her valise as if he picked it up by mistake or was carrying it as a courtesy to a lady stranger. His mistress's eyes slide in fright to the window where the Gévelot party sit watching. She grabs her case and heads for the next carriage.

Emma lets out a hoot. "Trying to pretend they're not travelling together."

"They must have been at his château," says Jules-Félix. "That's the only possible explanation for their both catching a train at Surdon, of all places."

"What a boor." Aimée sighs. "He might have had enough discretion to take his paramour to a hotel in Paris."

There are only two First-Class carriages, so unless the comte de Lévis-Mirepoix wants to be left behind at this wind-swept station, he has no choice but to open the door and climb in. "Gévelot." Greeting Jules-Félix with a bow. "Madame, always a pleasure." The comte has clearly decided to bluff it out, daring any of them to make a direct accusation, but he has a clammy look about him.

Emma introduces her companion, so he kisses Aimée's hand too.

Neither of the ladies asks whether that was Madame L'Heureux on the platform, but they do teasingly interrogate the comte about whether he feels restored by his time in the country.

"Ah, as always." He adjusts his monocle.

Having honoured his own marriage vows all these decades, Jules-Félix greatly relishes the adulterer's discomfort. The comte should have stuck to opera girls rather than seducing a married lady. And in his wife's own country house under the eyes of her own servants no less. Well, one way or another, word will spread now and he'll get his comeuppance. So much for the romance and anonymity of rail travel. Really, the two might as well have shown themselves off in the Lévis-Mirepoix coach on the afternoon drive through the Bois de Boulogne! It's a small world, and trains have only made it smaller.

"Shall I?"

"What's that?" Jules-Félix blinks at Emma.

"It's past noon, *mon cher*. Shall I open the hamper?"

"Certainly."

The comte is revealed to be travelling without so much as a crust, clearly because his mistress has the basket; the Gévelot party smirk at each other and Emma insists on sharing everything.

Perhaps to make up for the Christophles' guests not having been accommodated in the invalid carriage, the housekeeper at Gué aux Biches has packed them salt-marsh lamb accompanied by pommes au gratin. The Gévelots bicker amiably about whether the lamb really tastes any different from ordinary lamb, salted—but it's undeniably delicious. They open a jar of duck aiguillettes with caramelized apples and another of truffled pigs' trotters. For cheeses, they have Livarot, Brillat-Savarin, and Pont l'Évêque, and instead of cider, a pommeau made of Calvados mixed with fresh apple must.

His mood mellowed by the good lunch, Jules-Félix pours himself and the comte a glass each of a hearty burgundy. He doesn't feel obliged to make conversation, though; the two men shouldn't argue about politics in front of the ladies nor bore them by discussing army contracts. Instead, he folds the morning paper over and checks the tiny figures as he sips his wine.

"My husband's incapable of relaxation. He always has a watch in his hand, as it were," Emma complains.

"Well, time is gold, madame," the comte points out.

"Hear, hear," Jules-Félix murmurs without looking up.

"You men of business have your gazes so fixed on what's coming, the stock market and so forth, that you look right past the pleasures of the moment," Aimée scolds them. "And, really, once you're over the crest of the hill of life, what destination are you hurrying towards except, well ..."

Jules-Félix gives her a hard look. *The grave*, she means. Not a remark in very good taste for a dependent female to direct towards a man approaching seventy in whose house she camps.

Feeling a little churlish, he doesn't ask the ladies' permission before he gets out cigars for himself and the adulterous lord.

Jean Le Goff had his cold lunch in Rear Baggage half an hour back—potato stew and pickled herring, washed down with cider—*and* found time to trim his nails with his penknife; a single man has to keep up his standards. So now he runs for a piss and a quick coffee in the porters' room, pausing on the way to open the gate to the Third-Class platform area where a dozen passengers are chafing to be allowed onto the Express. Not to be confused with those in the local pen farther down the platform, resigned to waiting another hour for the cheaper train that stops forty times between Granville and Paris.

Checking Rear Second, Jean finds a young lady and gent having a rather intense conversation that they break off when he gets in. They hold out their tickets. Hers is green.

"Oh, but, mademoiselle," Jean says with an apologetic jerk of his thumb, "First Class is at the front."

Instead of thanking him, she lets out a small sigh. "I just wanted—I really had to get some typewriting done. I moved back here at Flers so as not to disturb the others."

He frowns, never yet having encountered a passenger sneaking into a *lower* class than the one for which he or she paid.

165

"Is there a rule against it?" she asks a little sharply.

No doubt Léon Mariette would be able to answer; that stickler reads the Company handbook as if it's a detective novel. Jean looks at the man pointedly; didn't she care about disturbing him?

That flusters the young lady. "This carriage was empty when I switched."

Ah—she's saying she's *not that kind of woman*.

"I got in at Briouze." The man's voice is hoarse, his French stiff, his accent American.

Jean examines his pink ticket. "Says here *Granville*." Again, odd—cheaters tend to carry tickets for journeys *shorter* than the ones they're taking.

"I got on at Granville, but I got in *here*, this carriage, at Briouze."

"Find the view better, do you?"

The American looks blank, bewildered.

"The view from this carriage?" Jean adds. Though it kills a joke to have to explain it.

Sarcasm is lost on this fellow. "No! I am not looking at anything." And then blood's suddenly trickling darkly down the man's lip, as if an invisible hand has dealt him a hard blow.

Jean recoils.

The American stares down at his white shirt. One poppy bloom of blood, another ...

A nosebleed, but heavier than Jean's ever seen, as if the fellow's tank has sprung a leak. Now, what is it you're meant to do for a nosebleed? Smelling salts, brandy? Guards are expected to have a medical kit always on them, though only old Mariette bothers.

"Let me." The young lady moves in, businesslike, lawn handkerchief at the ready. She presses the white lace-edged square to the unfortunate's nose and pinches it hard. He's shaking, sweating like a hog. "Breathe through your mouth, slowly."

"Is he dying?" If so, Jean needs to alert the Surdon stationmaster.

"Not at all. Such remarks are most unhelpful."

The American draws a long, shuddering breath.

"Don't speak," the lady orders him.

She seems to have the matter well in hand, so Jean swings the door open and drops lightly down.

One minute left. Just enough time to stick his head into Front Third. "Anyone who's boarded since Granville, hold up your tickets." Jean can check the colours, at least. Across from the Russian, a plump one with flaxen hair flaps about, saying she can't find hers—oldest trick in the book. Jean has a weakness for blondes, so he waits rather than issuing her a fine.

"Has he boarded, that the third deputy you mentioned? Where's he sitting?" the stocky girl asks.

He gives her a look; a nosy parker, this one. The Russian seems to think so too.

"What's all this about deputies?" a Breton woman wants to know.

"Today's train carries no fewer than three rulers of the nation, all from Orne," Jean boasts on behalf of the Express.

"Oh là là!"

The blonde produces her ticket just as a shout comes from Mariette on the platform: "Le Goff!"

So Jean jumps out, already sounding his warning whistle. Out of the corner of his eye he spots a red-faced man racing across a pasture towards the station, battered valise in hand. No, that poor dawdler's out of luck; he'll never catch this train in time.

12:15 p.m.

DEPART SURDON

Tarde venientibus ossa
(The late are left nothing but bones)

LATIN SAYING

Henry Tanner's dying. Halfway to Paris, in the arms of a stranger, her handkerchief scarlet with his blood. Dizzy, tingling from shoulders to fingertips, his heart a hammer clanging on the anvil of his chest—

"Sit up straight," Marcelle de Heredia instructs him.

She's switched back to English for his sake, he registers.

"Head down a little."

Henry tries to obey. "You must pardon me, miss—mademoiselle."

"Shh. There's no need. It could happen to anyone."

He's able to press her handkerchief to his own face, so she sits back in her corner of the carriage.

Gradually Henry feels his pulse decrease. He forces himself to break the silence and confess, "I'm bedevilled by nosebleeds at moments of . . . well, at random moments. But today, really, I've never felt anything like this."

"Nervous agitation can produce symptoms that perfectly mimic a heart attack."

His face scalds. "You must think me very timid for being thrown into such a state by the guard's questions."

"Not at all."

Marcelle's calm air of authority is too much to bear. Henry lifts away the clotted handkerchief experimentally and sniffs hard. The bleeding seems to have stopped.

She takes back her ruined handkerchief, showing no sign of disgust.

He manages to find his own handkerchief and mops his face with it. He finds he must level with her. "I've always had a particular dread of public transit."

One perfectly formed eyebrow tilts up. "Dread of an accident?"

"No, no. Of being challenged. Ejected."

She takes his meaning at once. "But that wouldn't happen in France," she protests.

Henry makes himself tell the story. "When I was only one year old, we were living in Virginia—one of the Southern states?" Yes, she seems to know what that means. "Before Christmas, my mother took me shopping in the nation's capital, Washington, DC."

Marcelle nods.

She probably knows all the capitals of the world, he realises. "A storm blew up, and we had to get home, but the streetcar was forbidden to us. My mother decided to pull a veil over her own head but leave my rather lighter face and my reddish curls exposed. In any event, a man on the streetcar stared at me, then yanked up my mother's veil and cried, *What have we here, it's a—*" Henry's throat locks on the slur. Well, Marcelle doesn't need him to say it.

Her expression is stony.

"So the driver slammed on the brakes and ordered us out in the snow. My mother had to carry me five miles home through the storm."

"Oh, Mr. Tanner." Her brown eyes are liquid with compassion.

Henry touches his chest. "Even now when I let myself think about it, heat surges here."

"Fury?"

"And hatred."

She doesn't cavil at the word. "Hatred of the driver? Or the man who insulted your mother?"

"Both of them, and the passengers—those who stood by and said nothing."

She nods. "Strange you remember it so well even though you were a baby."

"Oh, I'm afraid it's a false memory," he admits, "based on what my mother told me much later."

"Not false," Marcelle objects. "Handed down."

Henry likes that way of putting it, as if the pain is a family treasure. Or at least a useful tool.

"In situations when your agitation rises due to past pain," she murmurs, "perhaps you could remind yourself that this is not then? And that here is not there?"

Here is not there, Henry repeats in his head, *and this is not then.* This young lady is balm to his heart.

She suddenly changes the subject. "You asked what set me on the track of studying physiology. The truth is, it was the day my brother drowned."

"I'm so sorry to hear that." How funny that Henry's bleeding all over her seems to have made intimates of them. He watches, listening hard; he knows Marcelle's honouring him with this confidence.

"We were on holiday in Calais." She gestures north, across green fields. "I remember Papa on the strand trying to get the water out of Henri's lungs."

So Henry has the same name as her brother. "What age—"

"Thirteen. Henri, I mean. I was nine. I stood there staring at my father pounding and pounding my brother's back. I supposed that if I looked away, Henri would die."

His voice is hushed when he says, "You didn't look away."

"But he died anyway. He had already died," she corrects herself. "That was the day it seeded itself in me, the curiosity."

Could *curiosity* really be the English word she meant to choose?

"I wanted—no, I needed to know what the difference was between my brother after and before. What makes a body lie inert or move."

Henry's wondered something similar about the people in his paintings, because sometimes they're fake, made of flat pigment, but sometimes they flicker to life. He can't know in advance; he can only paint and wait and see.

"Thirteen seems so young to me now," Marcelle marvels.

"Your vantage point has changed."

"In another ten years, perhaps Henri will seem like a son to me."

Henry would very much like to know how wide the gap in years is between him and this lovely young Frenchwoman. "I've been working on a Lazarus," he mentions.

She looks startled; probably she didn't expect the American's work to be in the religious genre, even if he is a bishop's son.

"His resurrection," Henry spells out. "I'm envisaging Lazarus as a shadowy figure with a slab of light at his feet. I got the notion from a Rembrandt in which the only plausible source of illumination is the grave itself."

She nods, grasping what he means.

The radiance is of course the miracle-working love of Christ. The challenge for Henry is to paint this in such a realistic way that it'll move the doubters and even the godless. He doesn't say any of this, because Marcelle de Heredia may very well be one of those scientists who have left the consolations of religion behind.

173

"I suppose we always remember our dead in pictures," she murmurs. "Static, fixed, rather than moving. When in fact they're moving farther from us every day."

She checks her watch; it's well past noon. She takes out her lunch—a jar of cold potato soup and a chicken fricassee—and offers to share. Henry counters with his Camembert, rye bread, and apple tart, so they make a small feast of it all.

Blonska's somehow uneasy about this Mado Pelletier. Earlier in the day, she thought she had a good grasp on her type: naive, a little hotheaded, an idealist. Not unlike Blonska at the same age: a compulsive reader, a solitary, a freethinker who wouldn't stand for injustice.

Such an odd thing the girl demanded of the guard at Surdon, though. What could it matter to Mado Pelletier where on the train any of these deputies are to be found? Surely she can't mean to confront one of them on the platform or bang on his carriage door and shout, *Down with bourgeois pigs!*

Also, while the rest of the passengers have been eating what they've brought, Mado hasn't touched a bite of her lunch. Solidly built, she's clearly not one of these young people always in motion who have to be chivvied into eating. She's lifted her lunch bucket onto her lap now and she's looking down at it as if it's a tired, tearstained baby. Or a lover she fully expects to break her heart. Something sorrowful in her gaze but also elated.

No.

Shock catches in Blonska's throat.

Not that.

She rebukes herself for even thinking of such lurid possibilities. She's letting her imagination run wild. She's just tired from her cold night on the platform in Granville followed by this long, rattling journey.

It's not possible. For all her talk, Mado Pelletier would have to be unhinged to bring such a device onto a train.

Call it what it is: a *bomb.*

Except that it's not. It can't be. It's a lunch bucket, that's all. Probably warm cabbage soup in there.

But what's that Mado said, hours back? *Knowledge is not the only kind of power.*

Wait—no, no. There are those who take that terrible path, but they're wild-eyed madmen, aren't they? Past the reach of any appeal to reason or conscience, so intoxicated with conviction that their ears are sealed shut. Dynamitards who've despaired of fixing society and so have decided to smash it.

Mado's no killer, surely. Round-faced, only twenty-one. Full of righteous wrath, not ruthlessness; only passionate, not insane.

But no; Blonska realises she's fallen into the trap of conventional thinking—underestimating what a girl might become if she's sensitive enough to the wrongs of the world. Hasn't Mado spoken from the heart today, as if wanting someone, anyone, even some old Russian, to understand what she's about to do and why?

Blonska wonders when the bomber means to set it off, then, this possible-probable-almost-definite explosive device in a false lunch bucket. Will it be at the next station—will Mado do something to ignite it, then race out of the carriage to save herself? (But that would be a cold-blooded massacre, and Blonska can't believe it of this girl.) Or will she jump down onto the platform and hurl it through the window of one of the First-Class carriages that hold these deputies the guard spoke of? Blonska's mind is gelid with panic; she finds she can't remember the name of the next stop.

Victor Garnier chews his gritty lip. They've been running seven minutes behind ever since Briouze; they haven't been able to make up a single one.

Engine 721's not gasping yet, but two-thirds of the journey's done, so she's going to need water soon. Here comes the highest point of the whole route, Authieux-du-Puits, where the line dips under a picturesque bridge and plunges into the darkness of a tunnel. Once the train is past the spire of Sainte-Gauburge, Victor recognises the familiar line of the river Risle descending to cut the plateau. There's a trough coming up, a narrow reservoir of rainwater that runs for half a kilometre between the rails. He catches Guillaume's eye and tips an imaginary glass into his mouth, meaning *Time to give her a drink.*

The driver nods and nudges open the regulator to increase speed.

The Brits, as much as they lack all systematic thought, do

have a knack for practical inventions, and the railway water trough is the best of them. When Victor remembers all the time crew used to waste at country halts waiting for station men to wheel up a cistern and fill the tank by hose . . . imagine if he had to do that today, how many more minutes the Express would lose!

Here comes the white rectangular signboard with a black horizontal zigzag to mark the start of the unseen trough. Victor shoves on the handle to lower the scoop, letting the train's own forward thrust force the water up the pipe. He leans out to the side, his coat flapping up behind, the back of his hair lifting in the wind; he locks his eyes on the pointer attached to the tank's float. The split second the arrow reaches the fifteen-thousand-litre mark, he ducks back onto the footplate and yanks up the scoop.

Now the water jacket around the coal bunker is heavy with water, which adds maybe ten tons to the train's drag but should brew up enough steam to power them all the way to Montparnasse.

In Rear Third, Maurice Marland is yawning, eyes brimming. He looks up from his story, blinks hard, and reads the dozens of brand names pasted to the walls. He wants to ask the priest the time again, but the old man's head has tipped onto his chest. Maurice finds tiny children (such as the one still sprawled across her nurse's lap) sweet when they're asleep, but with old people, he always worries that they have died.

The nurse and the young missionary are chatting in Norman; Maurice can understand the odd word. He is picking up English already, as there are so many Anglos in this region. If his parents let him stay at school until he's sixteen, he could even learn Latin. He wants to learn all the languages there are in the world and all the skills and grow up to be of use, somehow.

The priest's head lolls back now, his open mouth like a skull's. His watch is dangling from his belt with the cover open. Maurice stands up and twists his neck around until he can read it—not touching it, so no one will think he's a thief. Half past twelve; another almost two hours until Dreux. (His papa waiting for him in the cart, the adventure over.)

A couple of people have unwrapped their food, so Maurice asks a man to get his schoolbag down from the net and takes out the squishy package in waxed paper. Hard-boiled eggs that Georges already shelled and salted. A barley bread sandwich, which he peels apart to see what's inside—a generous piece of horsemeat. A pear too! Maurice eats every bit as slowly as he can, to make it last, with sips of milk.

He reads more of his *Around the World* story, but his eyes keep closing, somehow heavy and fluttering at the same time, so he shuts them for just a minute ...

Now all the passengers around John Synge in Middle Third have pulled out their lukewarm cassoulets, garlic and sorrel sausage, cider and marc; the convivial fug thickens. He opens his own meagre bread and pâté. Annah Lamor is feeding crumbs of pastry to her monkey. It must have taken weeks for her to sail or steam from wherever in the world she started out, and John wonders if she brought the pet with her on the ship.

The oysterwoman drinks from a rattling flask that turns out—John can't stop himself from asking—to contain water fortified with rusty nails. She shucks her wares at a gouger's price of ten sous each, and Dois the delicatessen owner soothes the grumblers by sharing a whole boxful of nougats. The two students unbutton their stylish false collars to save them from stains before they eat cold chicken and share a cigarette with John.

Max Jacob says he has followed his brother into colonial administration, but he's studying law at the same time. "Couldn't decide between them, so I'm currently failing at both."

"My friend is in fact devilishly clever," Kiouaup says, touching a handkerchief to his lips.

"Something examinations inexplicably fail to measure," Max adds in a droll tone.

Kiouaup tells John that since he came to Paris eight years ago, his fees at the Colonial School have been covered as compensation for his father—the governor of a province called Kampong Tralach—having died for France.

John's not sure whether to congratulate or commiserate. "You must be eager to go home by now?"

Kiouaup shakes his elegant head. "In fact, I would prefer never to do so."

"He's an utter Parisian," Max puts in.

Yes, John's encountered many expatriates who seem to have what he lacks—bountiful confidence in the position they occupy in the city—because they know exactly what's drawn them to this crossroads of the modern world.

"Far more Parisian than I'll ever be," Max says out of the side of his mouth.

John's not sure he follows. "Because you're from Brittany?"

"No, because I was born foreign."

"Foreign to . . . France?" It's easier to ask probing questions when you won't meet any of these people again.

A theatrical sigh. "Foreign to life. I first tried to hang myself when I was thirteen."

John's eyebrows shoot up. It may no longer be a crime, but he's never heard anyone admit to such a thing. "D'you mind my asking—"

"Oh, it probably had something do with the Jew-baiters punching me in the head at school."

John cringes in sympathy.

"My father found me dangling by a necktie from the window hasp, and all he said was *Do stop fooling around*. My mother told me I could always kill myself later, which I found more helpful."

Oh, the poor boy. John's heart hurts for him.

"Just last spring, a dear friend, the genius of our *lycée*, threw himself in the river for love." Max's voice is suddenly husky, all sarcasm gone.

Annah Lamor is listening in. "Don't do it."

Max rolls his eyes.

"Don't let them win."

"Who, the tormentors? Very well, mademoiselle, I'll drink to that." Max leans across to clink his wine tumbler against hers, and John does the same with his water.

As the mood in the carriage turns more festive, John plucks up the courage to ask Annah where she does her act.

It turns out to be a damp cellar in Montparnasse called the Cabaret of Nothingness. John's heard about these death-themed cafés, very up to the minute, fin de siècle—which is a silly phrase, it strikes him now. Nothing changes just because a century is coming to an end. Besides, don't the Jews and Muslims and Hindus and Chinese have different calendars? (And the turning globe doesn't know or care what year it is.) But in recent years, the educated of Europe have started describing everything as *fin de siècle*; it's meant to capture a certain exhausted melancholy.

Annah's cabaret has coffins for tables, chandeliers made of fake bones, jokes about death on the walls, and two men dressed like monks droning plainchant. "I pour drinks, then the illusionist makes me rot."

"He makes you . . . I beg your pardon?"

"They see me like this"—she gestures impatiently at her orange dress. "Then in a bag thing, wrapped up—"

"A shroud?" John suggests. "A bag for a dead body?"

A nod. "Then all rotted. Then just a skeleton. He uses mirrors."

"Gracious me."

181

Annah wants to know how the Dubliner spends his own days.

He'd much rather listen than speak of himself, but he admits that he's been studying music in Cologne and is now taking courses in French and medieval literature at the Sorbonne.

"What's wrong with Ireland?" she demands.

"Nothing. It just rains a lot, and my lungs . . ."

"Rains in Paris too."

"Yes. Somehow it can be easier to be yourself abroad." Why is John attempting to explain his inchoate feelings to a creature of the night from the other side of the world?

"Because nobody knows you?"

He nods, glad of her quick understanding.

"Where you staying?"

He flushes, which is ridiculous; it's not as if this bird of paradise is going to hunt him down in his attic room. "Ah, just north of the cemetery."

"Montparnasse?"

When John nods, Max asks, "What's the only street in Paris that nobody lives on?"

This non sequitur makes him frown. "I don't quite—"

"You're close."

But John hasn't said anything.

"You're lodging around the corner from it, in fact. Rue Émile Richard, the one that cuts through the graveyard. Nobody *lives* there at all!"

Annah produces a professional ghostly cackle.

182

Max goes on. "You know it was students who named it that, as a joke?"

Now John's quite lost. "The street?"

"No, Montparnasse."

"Did they really?"

Max clenches his face around his monocle wisely. "In the sixteenth century the place was nothing more than a mound of quarry debris where our doubleted-and-hosed forebears got sloshed and read one another their poems."

John enjoys picturing that. He supposes the students wouldn't have been in anyone's way sprawling on a pile of rubble south of the city, and, more important, it wouldn't have cost them a sou. "Mount Parnassus, the hill sacred to the Muses?"

"Exactly!"

"You paint?" Annah suddenly asks him in an accusatory tone.

"Ah . . . do I look as if I do?"

A shrug. "Posh types, not real Montparnos, bourgeoisie playing at being bohemians—they're mostly painters. One time I model for a crazy one called Gauguin." She points up at the bulging net overhead. "That fiddle yours?"

John can't deny it.

"Play us something," Kiouaup orders merrily.

He throws up his hands. "Pardon me, I can't."

Max claps. "You must, you must. I'd accompany you if we had a piano."

"No, truly, I have a horror of performing," John confesses. "That's why I gave up music—all those eyes and ears on me."

Annah snorts, and the plumes in her hat shimmy. "People look at me anyway, even if I just walk down the street. Last time I'm in Brittany, they call me a witch and throw stones!"

John grimaces at that.

An unsmiling laugh. "Better to show myself and get paid, I say." The monkey's balanced on her shoulder; she feeds it a currant. The creature scratches its belly, its sardonic face a pagan mask.

Annah asks to borrow the fiddle if John won't play.

"Certainly!" He lifts it down for her.

She plays an uneven, skipping tune with something sad about it—a *danse macabre*, John thinks. A discarded wine bottle rolls to and fro across the floor.

He taps along and looks out the window to hide his feelings. He longs to wrap Annah in his arms and save her from the merciless world.

He sees a man inching his way along the edge of a field, pulling a cart as if he's a beast of burden. With a twinge in his gut John remembers, as a boy, begging his mother not to let his brother evict their poor tenants. She asked, *If they don't pay, what do you propose to live on?*

He can't tell Annah that story. She's already guessed that he's a posh (if broke) bourgeois, not a *real Montparno*.

Here's the famous tower of Verneuil-sur-Avre, tapering like a candle. Annah won't be interested in John's thoughts on the Flamboyant Gothic style, and the tower's already gone by.

As the others in Front Third munch away like sheep, Mado sits exalted. Three deputies on the Express now. That's not just luck. What was the line old Blonska quoted? *No accidents, only fate misnamed.* After twenty-one years of muddling along through circumstances of the most arbitrary, thwarting kind, Mado finally finds herself believing in something like destiny. No gods, no angels, but something—the spirit of history?—is cheering her on.

Is this the perfect moment? The very important guests are gathered. If three members of parliament are in the First-Class carriages on the other side of this wall, what can Mado be waiting for?

The lunch bucket stands on her thighs; she's holding it upright with an iron grip. She tries to think of anything else that could make the disaster huger, more memorable in its effects. If the train's going through a tunnel, will the explosion wreck the stonework? Or she could do it when they're next passing over a bridge, when the detonation might toss into the river not only the whole reptilian body of the train but also the bridge itself, leaving the main railway line to the west out of commission.

Beside her, the blonde, Cécile Langlois, shifts uncomfortably and rubs her bulging belly.

It doesn't matter, Mado reminds herself, looking away. *Or, rather, this woman matters, of course—we all matter—but the revolution matters more.*

Months ago Mado came to terms with this. Her own death is required of her today, as are the deaths of even innocents, like this blonde probably is, and distinctly good people, like Blonska. The same goes for just about all the passengers and workers crammed onto this train. They may not deserve to die, but what has deserving ever had to do with death? Wars already eat up so many of the poor, as do mining and factory accidents, famines and diseases, all the poisons that run through the veins of France. Better to die importantly, even gloriously, so the next generation can truly live, no? Better to be blown sky-high in a wreck that will never be forgotten, that will give the powers that be an urgent warning of a new world on its way . . .

Mado sings that song in her head, the one from the cabaret the other night:

> *What does it matter*
> *If we fail, if we fall,*
> *Without seeing the future?*
> *The kids will have it all.*
> "Not eating?"

She stares at her neighbour.

The man in the bowler hat is gnawing on the last of a leg of mutton. "Aren't you having yours?"

Mado's holding the handle of her lunch bucket so hard, it burns like a brand. "I'm not hungry."

"Huh! Got anything nice in there?"

She turns her gaze away from him—

Towards old Blonska, whose eyes in their wrinkled pouches

are burning weirdly. Who drops her head, too fast, and works her clacking needles.

And Mado realises with a prickle of shock that the old woman's somehow guessed.

Heart goes *bam-bam*. Is Blonska planning to wait till they stop next, at Dreux, and screech for the gendarmes? But it really will make no difference how many come running. (Mado hates all police, because their main job is to stop those who have nothing from taking anything from those who've always hogged everything.)

All the power is in these short, thick fingers of hers, Mado reminds herself. She slides her eyes towards Blonska's bent, silvery head. *Before anyone lays a hand on me, I can blow us all to kingdom come.*

How can Blonska, with all the benefit of age and experience, have lost command of her expression? All she needed to do was keep her face calm, her look cool. Now the girl's guessed that Blonska knows, which makes the situation even more dangerous.

Terror has Blonska in its grip. She's in the thrall of the object itself, the lunch bucket that's not a lunch bucket. (Unless it really is? She still longs to be ridiculously wrong about this.) Her breath is coming fast and shallow, and wet's broken out on her upper lip. *Please,* she finds herself begging the God she doesn't believe in. *Not today.*

Blonska made her funeral arrangements years ago, but now that the end is nearing in a rush, she's not ready. That interests the analytical part of her mind, the little clock that ticks on through the storm of panic: So those in chronic pain with no family to cling to them are just as unwilling to go as those who have youth, beauty, health, and wealth. It seems life, in any form, is too sweet to surrender. Blonska thinks of all the books she's left unread.

And of all the other passengers—these already familiar faces in Front Third and those strangers crowded in all the other carriages. The kind maid Madame Baudin; the bumptious oysterwoman; the Granvillais with the bowler hat; the soldier; this poor Cécile Langlois, weighed down by her bump.

Mado Pelletier is a murderous madwoman, Blonska reminds herself. But even through this fog of terror, she's having trouble hating the girl. What grips her is more like a painful sympathy. Regret, even guilt, that Blonska or someone like her didn't come across the girl years ago, spot her talents, and enlist her help to mend the world. Instead this young zealot has come to the appalling conclusion that the best use she can make of her life is to throw it like a flaming spear.

Because Blonska's guessed something else—there's one part of the deranged plan that's clear to her. Mado Pelletier has no intention of running away. What a paradox—a killing in which the first victim will be the killer. Blonska's heard of such a possibility only once before. One of the Nihilists who blew up the czar in St. Petersburg more than a dozen years ago was killed in the blast—some said accidentally, but others said intentionally, offering himself like a lit match to the kindling. Mado Pelletier seems of that kind. She won't do anything to these passengers that she wouldn't do to herself. She has the glow of a warrior going into battle.

If Mado doesn't mean to save herself, Blonska realises, the detonation doesn't even have to be at a station. Blonska doesn't know the technicalities but presumes the girl can set off her device at any moment.

She swallows hard; a choking sensation. *What to do?*

There's no easy way to summon a guard until Dreux.

If Blonska makes any sudden move—lunging in her stiff way to grab the lunch bucket—well, it will only prompt its owner to detonate it at once.

Should Blonska shout out her more-than-suspicions to the other occupants of Front Third? No; even if she somehow managed to convince them right away, that too would force Mado's hand.

Is there some way for her to tell the other passengers without Mado knowing so they could all act at the same moment, pinning Mado down and getting the lunch bucket from her, perhaps hurling it out the window? But no—to fail to hear them plotting, the girl would need to be in an enchanted sleep.

The chink in the armour of most criminals is their need to make a getaway. If Mado Pelletier is, in fact, prepared—no, eager—to die . . . then she's invincible.

Nothing. For now, that seems the safest thing to do. Blonska's trapped in her knowledge, unable to act.

Strangely, she finds she doesn't want Mado Pelletier hurt. Or arrested, even. If the police collar her, she'll be excoriated in the papers, put on trial, and guillotined like those other anarchists, and in turn she'll inspire new martyrs. No, what Blonska wants is to call a halt. Now, as they glide through the verdant landscape; now, when no crime has been committed yet, when in fact nothing has happened. If only Blonska could freeze time to make a little breathing space, take the girl's hand, and say, *Please, for all our sakes, hear me out . . .* is there a brilliant argument that could dissuade Mado, a magic word that could soften her heart? Blonska casts her mind back to when she was twenty-one, with all the gifts and weaknesses of that age. She was so all-or-nothing, so very stubborn, so akin to this French youngster. If Blonska had found herself on the death track, what might have steered her off it?

She finds she can't think of a single thing to say to the girl. The bomb in its slim metal bucket seems to suck all the words out of her head.

The little round blonde beside Mado lets out a groan. Cécile's head tips up and presses against the shoulders of the man behind her so her straw hat is driven forward over her eyes.

"Hey!" he objects.

She moans, thrusts out the ball of her belly, and shoves both fists into the small of her back.

Blonska is filled with a new exhaustion. "Madame— Cécile, *ma chère*," she murmurs, "could it be that your time has come?"

"Not till I get to Paris!"

Half the passengers in Front Third have caught that exchange, and it quickly spreads to the other half. Women tut and sigh or cross themselves. Another whimper from Cécile as she arches sharply. The man sitting back to back with her stands up, looking alarmed. Mado shrinks away on the bench and turns her face to the window.

Whenever Blonska steps into the fetid apartments of those who need her help, she becomes paralysed for a moment. Her habit is to take a long breath and ask herself what the most urgent matter is, however small, then tackle that. Right now she can't think of anything to do about what's in that lunch bucket, so she's going to focus on what she knows how to do.

She puts her hands on Cécile's knees, only a few centimetres from her own. "Tell me, how long has your back been hurting?"

A sob. "Just today. On and off for hours, but it's getting much worse now."

A sure sign, and one she hid as long as possible so she'd be allowed make her trip. Blonska sighs. First things first— she must try to get this poor creature off this cursed train. "We'll set you down at Dreux shortly, and the station guard will call a midwife."

Struggling to catch her breath, Cécile protests, "My sister's expecting me."

"We make plans, and the gods laugh." By *the gods*, she means the random forces that govern human lives as casually

191

as the tide shakes up sand in a rock pool, the forces that have put these people in a railway carriage with a bomber who means to kill them all. "I'd say you'll be having your baby at Dreux."

"I will *not!*" Cécile writhes on the bench, her hair escaping her hat like chaff. "What do you know?"

Blonska doesn't take this personally; she's familiar with the rage of women enduring these pangs. "From the births I've seen—"

A tear plummets down Cécile's red face. "I tell you, I can hold on till Paris."

Some of the passengers have looked away as if trying not to hear, but others are enjoying the drama. "Not up to you, *ma puce*, is it?" asks Madame Baudin.

"My girl came early and my boy late," remarks another woman.

"Haven't you heard the proverb?" That's the oysterwoman speaking over her shoulder from the next bench. "*No one's born till their time, nor dies neither*. Well, it must be this one's time."

"Who said anything about dying?" Furious, the words that spray from Cécile's mouth.

"We're here." That's Mado, in a strange voice.

Blonska rubs her eyes. Could the girl mean that they'll all help, even her?

But Mado gestures at the window. "Dreux."

HALT DREUX

Those who kiss too much
will miss the train.

FRENCH PROVERB

O n the footplate, the two rollers pull their goggles off to rub some blood back into the circles of compressed flesh. Guillaume's eyes are ringed with soot, as they always are towards the end of a long day; Victor knows his own are too. "Ten minutes late, and no prospect of making up any of those minutes here," Guillaume says hoarsely.

Victor nods, scanning the passengers milling about like cockroaches. The bread and sausage at Surdon has worn off, and he's hungry again, but his need to empty his bowels is more pressing.

He can't risk nipping to the porters' room; rollers mustn't stir from the footplate during the journey, and Mariette would write him up for *deserting his post*. So he brushes past

Guillaume to get to the far side and lets himself drop to the gravelled track. He unbuttons his trousers and squats, leaning one hand on a gigantic wheel. Hardly safe, but if he goes farther off, a passenger might see him out the window, and anyway, the clock's a-ticking. Sudden autumnal sunlight dazzles him.

Nothing. Constipation, Victor's old complaint. *Come on, man!*

Above him on the footplate, the scratch of the shovel; is his restless mate tidying up a few fallen cinders?

"On my way!" Victor holds his breath and strains. Halfway out, what feels like a lump of stone. Heaves again. The familiar burn of his hole.

"Seventy-eight kilometres to go," Guillaume says from overhead, "which usually takes us an hour and forty, but you know what? I bet we could shave ten minutes off that."

Victor mulls that over, shaking his arse to throw off the hard turd.

"It's a straight run, no twisty bits or big hills to slow us …"

He squeezes himself shut and steps well away, pulling up his drawers. He's surprised Guillaume wants to risk his impeccable record by breaking the rule against speeding.

But there's such a thing as a careful dash—as opposed to a rash dash—and if the best driver in the Company thinks it's safe to go a touch over, who's his stoker to doubt him? *It might even be safer, for the sake of catching up,* Victor tells himself as he fumbles with his buttons, because the closer that trains keep to their posted schedules, the less likely it is that a signalling error will cause one of them to run into another. Besides, if the bosses really didn't condone speeding, they wouldn't offer an extra month of pay in December for keeping to the schedule; the only logical explanation is that the Company, like some hypocritical father, would rather have it done tacitly.

So Victor climbs back onto the footplate and says, "All right, I'm with you. Let's shave the ten minutes off."

Guillaume nods, grinning.

"We won't let the buggers rob us of our Christmas money."

"No, we won't." Sun haloing the man's handsome face. "Are we masters of the rails?"

"We are!"

A bang on the side wall of Rear Baggage. Jean takes a last suck on his pipe. He throws open the door, and golden afternoon light pokes him in the eyes. "Surdon already?"

"Dreux," Léon Mariette corrects him.

"Slip of the tongue."

Accusatory: "You've been napping?"

"No, just having a smoke." Jean counts the day-trippers lining up to squeeze onto the train for their return to Paris. Dreux has a station buffet, so passengers who haven't eaten since Granville are dashing to buy a plate of late lunch. He grabs an armful of parcels from Mariette to stack in his van.

"Careful! And I told you before, you mustn't smoke in here—the post will smell of it."

"Everything that goes by rail reeks of coal anyway."

The lines around the senior guard's mouth deepen. "Have you checked everyone's tickets?"

"Ah . . . I believe so." The truth is, Jean doesn't bother with the people in First Class if they're dressed well; he bets that if they can afford the clothes, they can afford the tickets. "I see a passenger who needs me, *if* you don't mind?"

He canters down to Front Third, where that crookbacked Russian's beckoning from the open brown door. "What's the matter, madame?"

"Help us." Her voice comes out small and tight. "Here, in our carriage, there's a woman in distress. But first, I must tell you—"

He shoves past her, clumsy with haste, because the Express is behind already.

This big-bellied, scarlet-cheeked blonde squirming on the bench, Madame Langlois, is a stubborn creature. In between groans, she argues and won't hear of getting off the train: "I don't know a soul in Dreux."

"But you need a doctor," Jean insists.

"Haven't you sent for one?" a man in a bowler hat barks at him.

"The minute she'll kindly disembark, I'll put her in the care of the stationmaster and he'll call for medical attention." Jean can't go haring off to do that himself because it would cause further delay.

"Paris," Madame Langlois says between pants, "I must get to Paris."

There's a ring cutting into her fat finger, but Jean's not fooled. The capital is where her kind go for its public assistance and free medical care and anonymity. (He's heard of a hospital just west of Montparnasse at Denfert-Rochereau with a turntable in the outer wall where you can place a newborn; you put it in a box there, spin the wheel, ring the bell, and walk away before the nun comes.)

The collar-and-tie girl hasn't spoken before, but now she turns a steely gaze on him and says, "Get her off this train."

The Russian throws her a startled glance.

Jean bristles at the order; who does the creature think she is?

The woman in labour grips the planks of the bench and grimaces at him. "Don't you dare manhandle me."

"Do it," the Russian urges, "but gently."

"Hurry up!" That's collar-and-tie.

Jean spells it out to the group. "I'm not permitted to lay a hand on anyone. The Company could be fined, and I could be had up in court for assault."

Collar-and-tie girl is gripping her lunch bucket as if she'd like to club him with it.

"I'm afraid she's just going to have to sit tight."

He's already out on the steps when the Russian's cry arrests him. "Please!" Framed in the doorway with her skewed spine, her face piteous.

"Madame, what do you expect me to—"

She cuts him off. "Listen, monsieur, you must clear this carriage." Throws a glance over her shoulder. "I very much suspect—I've reason to believe—"

The short-haired girl is right beside her. "What are you saying, Blonska?"

Not another word from the Russian. Their stares lock.

Jean never ceases to marvel at how feuds about such petty matters as smells or windows can build up over the course of a long journey.

"Spit it out," the girl says. She does something odd then— she holds up her lunch bucket as if offering it to the older woman.

Is that what this bad blood's about, Jean wonders—food? Does the younger one have something tasty in there she won't share?

Still no answer from the Russian.

Collar-and-tie sways back a little and nods at the platform. "Get down yourself if you like. I won't stop you."

The Russian doesn't move. Jean's losing patience with this pair.

From the blonde behind them, a guttural sound of pain. Both women turn their heads.

And Jean takes the opportunity to jump down and head towards a barrow of parcels he's just spotted.

———

Marcelle de Heredia has climbed out of Rear Second for a little air, as the afternoon's turned so lovely. Also to find the ladies' water closet (always hidden away at the back of the station, if there's one at all) and to throw away the sodden, scarlet handkerchief that now seems to be composed less of cotton than of Henry Tanner's blood. These days every public building has three rubbish bins—one for the reclaiming of paper and cloth, the next for glass, ceramics, and oyster shells, and the last for perishables, which is where she drops the handkerchief.

"Mademoiselle de Heredia?"

She flinches, recognising the voice. It's the racing-car driver's wife, heading from the water closet straight to Marcelle, smoothing down her vivid green skirts.

She's frozen like a rabbit. "Madame Levassor—Sarazin-Levassor, I mean—"

"As we came into Dreux," the lady remarks airily, "I spotted one of our models."

Marcelle blinks, unnerved. "Oh, one of your firm's?" *Can this woman really have hurried down the platform just to chat about automobiles?*

Two hectic spots on the handsome face; she has the same lovely features as her sickly daughter, just more set, with those hieratic hummingbird masks dangling. She stands very close to Marcelle, eyes on a hotel across the street. "Yes, our make is called Panhard and Levassor."

"Gracious." Marcelle's mind is spinning. "I'd have thought a motorcar of any kind is a rare sight this far from Paris."

"Indeed, though Benzes are getting more common. When my husband and I are driving in the country, the yokels sometimes turn in disgust and shout, *Get a horse!*"

Marcelle manages a laugh. "I thought I saw a steam-powered tricycle back at Surdon." She's attempting to keep the conversation on safe ground. But then she understands that Louise Sarazin-Levassor is trying to work up to something, the way a runner jogs on the spot before a sprint. So Marcelle broaches the subject: "Madame, truly, I apologize again for what I said earlier—"

"No, no, it's I who must beg your pardon, mademoiselle. I'm sure your intentions were kind." She gazes up into a tree whose yellow leaves are blackening at the edges. "I called you stupid, which was cruel of me—"

"No, no—"

"Cruel *and* inaccurate, because I can tell you do know what you're talking about."

"How?" Marcelle sputters.

"I'm acquainted with quite a few scientists, and you have the unmistakable air of one."

She's silenced, and quite miserable.

"So. The special test you suggested, the one for *milkiness*." Louise Sarazin-Levassor forces out the syllables.

Shrinking from the word, Marcelle nods.

"It's been stuck in my head all day. How can blood be milky?"

Marcelle feels her gorge rise. Is it too late to lie and claim she didn't mean anything at all and even if she did, she was probably wrong?

She tries to answer as plainly as she would in the laboratory if her tutor were testing her. "Under the microscope . . .

they'd look for whiteness, by which they mean a preponderance of colourless cells."

"And whatever does it—what might it mean if they were to find this quality in Jeanne's blood?" The mother's voice trips over the girl's name.

"Well. For instance, there's an abnormality knows as leukaemia." This is gobbledygook to a layperson. "Or some nickname it *white blood*. I would have expected your daughter's doctor to . . ." *What, you're daring to criticize a physician now?* "He might like to recommend the test, just to rule it out."

The lady nods, and so does Marcelle, as if both of them believe the test will definitely rule that out. "I've never heard of it," Louise Sarazin-Levassor says, "so it must be rather rare."

Marcelle keeps nodding as if she agrees.

"And if . . . in the event that a person did have that, this *white blood*—what a curious name, when blood's so very red, the reddest thing there is—what I mean is, I suppose what I'm asking is, what might the course of treatment be?"

This is the question Marcelle's been dreading. If she's not willing to be brutally blunt and say, *There is none*, why did she ever let the conversation reach this cliff edge? "My area of study is physiology. I really know nothing about medicine."

"You know more than me, mademoiselle. You've heard of this *white blood*, at least."

Every time the other woman pronounces the term, it sounds more bizarre to Marcelle. As if it's possible for a human body to run on pure, colourless liquid, like milk or sap or light. She squirms. "There are ways of easing each symptom. I've heard of doctors using quinine for the fever that often accompanies the, ah, complaint." A euphemism for *disease*. "Morphine can be useful in case of bowel troubles . . . I believe a solution of arsenic can help," she adds weakly. *Help for a while*, she doesn't add, *for a few months of remission*. This isn't an illness with which one lives long.

Louise Sarazin-Levassor's face is quite flat.

"All I'm suggesting is that you speak to the doctor."

She nods, her eyes on a passing cyclist. "Well, we'd better not miss our train. Enjoy the rest of the journey, mademoiselle."

"You too," Marcelle manages hoarsely.

So they smile as they part in the way that ladies are trained to do, no matter the circumstances.

And Marcelle frantically wonders whether the mother will speak to the doctor, and whether the doctor will order the test, and what the test will reveal, and what will happen to Jeanne Sarazin-Levassor. Marcelle's unlikely ever to learn the end of the story. They're like *ships that pass in the night*, as the old poem puts it, but people could just as easily say, *Like strangers on a train*.

Not wanting to use the pot in front of Anna or his grandson, Albert Christophle has had to hold his water till Dreux, but he's hurrying along the side of the station now. (Passing a prostitute and her customer going at it with efficient vigour against the wall, both their stylish fedoras bobbing.)

When Albert reaches the urinal, there's a dark green steel screen around it and a railwayman leaning in a shaft of sun, having a smoke. A porter, perhaps, or a ticket collector? Not particularly young, not particularly good-looking; bushy dark hair from cheeks to throat.

The moment the men's glances meet, Christophle goes from slightly hard to rather hard. His bladder is still full, but all at once it's no longer urgent because the pressing matter is his excitement. He's at half-mast already.

He's never yet waded into real danger; with each stranger, he possesses the knack of knowing whether it'll be a yes or a no, a flirtatious *All right, monsieur* or a threatening *Casse-toi!* This one feels safe enough, so Albert rummages around in his waistcoat pocket. He can still tell all the coins apart by feel, though it's been forty years since anything but high-denomination banknotes mattered to him. He plucks out five francs in silver (bearing the draped personifications of liberty, equality, and fraternity). Some think it vulgar to show cash up front, and there's always the risk of having it snatched, but that's insignificant beside the risk of being seen by a gendarme. Also, the truth is, a little bit of danger is what's making Albert get so stiff.

Everything about these encounters is so entirely unlike performing what doctors term *marital relations* in his wife's bedroom—not that there's been any call for that in almost two years, given her health, nor any prospect that he will need to resume those duties. No, this place, the urinous tang as he steps into the other man's moving shadow, the quiver of

fear, the grin exchanged at the same moment as the coin . . .
this is why Albert's getting harder and harder as he unbuttons his suspenders and drops his trousers, his old cock protruding from his billowing starched shirt. He reaches for the
railwayman, who's one great mass of black fuzz, and they're
sword-fighting already, the man's long, slightly skewed weapon
frotting and nuzzling Albert's like enemies and friends at
once, and—*Oh, nom de Dieu*—there's so little time to savour
this, no time for more than one hard kiss of that furry face
pungent with tobacco, because the Express is about to leave.
So he finds the cleft underneath and shoves himself through
the damp track between the man's hairy thighs.

Without a word, the fellow clamps his legs around Albert
like a vise. There's barely room for Albert's cock between the
fellow's muscular legs, the squeezing, friction, but he keeps
jamming through that tight alley as if dynamiting a moun-
tain. He pulls the railwayman's crooked member against his
own pale belly—the heat of it!—and pumps it like a sailor
trying not to drown.

No sound but their frantic breathing, then in the distance,
the guard's piping whistle—the first or the final warning?
There can't possibly be enough time for a man of Albert's age
to finish now, so he should probably give up on the attempt,
wrench himself away, and run. There's a risk that he'll be
caught here at the back of the station by whoever's been sent
off to fetch this very important passenger, in which case the
Christophle name will crash down like a chandelier. So how
can it possibly be worth the candle for Albert to stay locked

to this spot, this still point in a whirling world, rocking and jarring and gasping, doing this and nothing but this, willing to throw his whole life on the bonfire for this raw bliss—

The other man blows first, and that hot splatter on Albert's belly is what does it, pushing him over the edge of sensation and lighting up his skull like fireworks with an almighty *Yes*.

An interrogative call from the driver's steam whistle. In response, the station agent's handbell gives permission to leave.

Albert hauls up his trousers and braces as he runs off without a glance behind, stuffs in his shirt, buttons his coat. The final whistle from the guard in the front van, and as Albert rounds the building, the glinting train is pulling out, but he's still got it, sixty-five be damned. Albert grabs the door handle with his right hand and yanks himself up and in, shaking, laughing.

"Grandpapa!" André, not so much relieved to see him as thrilled by the daring.

Albert's right arm burns. He's ready with his story (the toilets were occupied—no, locked, that's better), but his wife, lying flat behind her drapes with eyes half shut, shows no sign of having noticed his absence. Clearly Anna didn't send anyone to fetch him. Would she have thought to complain only when they got to Montparnasse and he wasn't there to help her disembark? Really, doesn't Albert matter to her at all?

Right now he doesn't care. His need to empty his bladder has come back rather painfully, but he doesn't give a fig about that either.

The hamper's open, Albert sees, the contents disarrayed. "Shall we have a bite of lunch?"

Anna waves that away with revulsion.

"I ate things while you were gone," André admits to his grandfather. "I couldn't wait."

Albert knows that children should be taught to defer gratification, but he murmurs, "Quite right." He takes a plate and puts a confit duck leg on it, and some rabbit with morels, and a generous helping of creamed leeks.

Almost sweeter than the coupling itself, this aftermath. Like a clear blue sky inside his head. The train gathers speed, and Albert lurches. He drops into a chair, steadying his plate, and feels the stickiness of a nameless man's spend gluing his shirt to his middle, a secret so thrilling it half rouses him again.

2:30 p.m.
DEPART DREUX

They didn't last long. That's how it is—
The loveliest days are the shortest.

HENRI MURGER,
SCENES OF BOHEMIAN LIFE (1851)

*E*very *fine day has its cloud*, as the saying has it. The skies draw in—dark to the train's left, still bright to her right—and rain starts to fall.

Less than an hour and a half to Paris, the lodestone to which we're unswervingly attracted. The land begins to slope up. Engine 721's rollers know every inch of the route and they feel the increasing effort it takes as gravity drags on her, slowing her further.

Against her will, the train carries death in her belly. Her only power is motion. She didn't choose this track; all she can do is keep going down it.

⸻

Every time Cécile Langlois moans on the bench beside her, Mado reminds herself she doesn't care. There's no time left for sentimentality. *The pigheaded fool brought this on herself by refusing to get down at Dreux.*

Madame Baudin demanded every cloak and shawl to make the poor creature a nest on the floor, but Blonska argued that the bench is rather less dirty. These two women are encouraging Cécile through each protracted pang, but the other passengers have tried to get as far from Cécile as they can—especially the men, with their appalled, averted faces. Except Mado, who's stayed in her seat with her feet planted, pressing her shoulder blades against the narrow wooden divider.

She's ignoring her own aching bladder, and the heavy rag roll that may well be leaking red into her skirt by now, and her hunger and thirst. She keeps her eyes half open in case the Russian tries something rash, such as whispering a warning to Madame Baudin or making a lunge for the lunch bucket in Mado's lap.

But Blonska—having perversely stayed in this hellhole of a carriage when Mado gave her a choice at Dreux—seems to be concentrating fully on her task. *Meddling busybody!* Clearly the Russian means to die as she's lived, trying to improve her little stinking corner of the world.

Rain begins to pebble the window. Mado's plan is quite clear in her mind now: She's going to set off her bomb as the train pulls into Montparnasse.

How can it have taken her so long to realise that there could be no better moment, no more perfect target? Her bomb would be wasted on a bare stretch of landscape or a country station. It stands to reason an explosion will cause the greatest damage in a densely built-up area, but what's even more important is the symbolism of the gesture. Paris is the furnace that powers the whole country—in fact, the whole French Empire, from Guiana to Indochina to Quebec. Paris is the beating heart of every form of hateful power: government by corruption and surveillance, church, military, capital, trade, industry ... The city's name stands for exploitation and it jingles like money. Paris (and the rancid Pelletier greengrocery at the heart of it) contains all Mado hates. Soon the Express is going to shoot like an arrow into the belly of the cancerous beast. That's the moment Mado will blow it up with a boom and a blaze.

She hopes to be the first to die, then those sitting near her: Blonska, Cécile, Cécile's tiny passenger. (*Does it count as death if it happens before birth?*) Probably everyone in Front Third as well as those in the private carriage, and perhaps also the crew and the hundred-odd passengers, plus station staff, even passersby on the streets. The moment Mado inverts her lunch bucket, she'll make phoenixes of them all. Impossible to predict the mayhem, how the rolling cars may leap, ride up on each other, telescope, wrench, rip, or burn.

Cécile arches with a groan, gasps, subsides. Smears her teary face. "Such a bad start in life," she laments.

"Nonsense," Blonska murmurs.

"No father, no home. Papa told me to leave it in one of the public orphanages in Paris."

"You can't be sure what'll happen," says the Russian. "Many a long, good life has had a rough start. Who knows what this child will grow up to be? The possibilities are infinite."

Listening despite herself, Mado scoffs. *Infinite possibilities for pain.*

"Think of the people on this train," Blonska urges the suffering woman, "what frail mites they were when they were born. How little they could have predicted the paths they've taken. The paths that *still* lie ahead. All the good they could still do."

Mado turns her head to meet Blonska's eyes in their nests of wrinkles. She tells her wordlessly, *You can't stop this.*

Here comes the next pang, and Cécile wails and lashes about.

Mado won't let herself be distracted. She's guarding her fury like a candle flame.

———

The rain's given the tracks a silvery, slippery sheen, and with a nod, Guillaume allows Victor to release a little sand onto them, for grip.

Pushing on, trying to catch those lost minutes. (Guillaume pictures them like rabbits, warm and bleeding in his grasp.) He finds his pulse is hitching and skipping. He's never given the Company any trouble in twenty-one years. He'll be riding the rails for another two decades—if his strength holds out.

Victor gets worked up about the unfairness of shifting the retirement age from fifty to fifty-five, but Guillaume can't find it in himself to object. What would he be doing if not this? He has no dream of keeping a few cows under his own apple trees and tasting his own butter and cider. And what would he find to say to Françoise if he had all day to say it in? No, this is the best job in the world until the day it might happen to kill him.

Here comes the ring of train tracks known as the Great Belt that encircles the capital's ever-swelling belly. For railwaymen, Paris starts here. Shooting through the low pink-and-white station of Versailles Chantier is when Guillaume always registers that he's back and checks his watch. Today, it's 3:43; his eyes sting with shame. The stationmaster here will already have directed the telegraph woman to wire HQ that the Paris Express is running nearly eight minutes behind. The speed Guillaume and Victor have maintained since Dreux has not managed to make up any of the owing minutes.

If he pushes Engine 721 from the low fifties per hour into the sixties, maybe he could shave four minutes off the missing eight and get in at 3:59, the right side of four o'clock. Surely arriving at 3:59 couldn't count as enough of a delay to drag down the crew's Christmas pay? Guillaume doesn't need to ask Victor; he trusts his mate will always back him. So he gives her more steam, urging her on like a racehorse.

A signal box ahead marks a set of double compound points, where each train is offered four routes. Rules say to use the regulator to slow down here, so Guillaume does, but he shifts the handle only ninety degrees, so as soon as they're past the branching tracks, he can push the speed back up, up, up. She's going faster than she should, but who on a train or watching it pass can be quite sure of its speed? Even her driver can make that calculation only by counting over the course of a minute, using his watch, and what driver on the final stretch into Paris possibly has time for that?

Engine 721 rockets on. Ah, they're so near home, she smells the stable now . . .

Louise Sarazin-Levassor leans back on the velvet upholstery, staring out the window. Rain, as if the sky is weeping. Her sideways gaze touches on her daughter playing with the spaniel, but lightly; Jeanne is the kind of sensitive girl who feels it like a touch if someone's staring.

What was the scientific name for it again? *White blood* is all Louise remembers. *White blood* is what she'll have to say to the doctor. Why does a disease need a nickname, as if it's a pet? The kind of disease that's every parent's nightmare, making straight for Jeanne, inexorably, faster and faster—

Monsieur Bienvenüe's getting very animated as the train nears the capital. Clearly he wants to tell the Levassors something about the important meeting for which he's cut his holiday short. "I've prepared a proposal . . . well, let me start by asking you how many horse-drawn cabs ply their trade in Paris, would you say?"

Preoccupied with the pallor of her daughter's downy cheek, Louise doesn't answer.

"There must be hundreds," Émile guesses. "Over a thousand?"

"Ten thousand, monsieur."

"No wonder the streets reek!"

"Each typically carrying just one or two passengers wealthy enough to hire a cab," says Bienvenüe, "while the footsore poor lose half their day plodding into town to work and out again because they can't even afford the fare for a bus, tram, or train. Well, I want to do away with them all."

Louise blinks. "The poor?"

"The cabs—in fact, the traffic in general. Let's go underground, I say. A system of electrified trains no more than twenty metres beneath our feet!"

Émile's indulgent smile suggests this is a harebrained scheme. "With some well-appointed First-Class carriages in your subterranean kingdom, I hope?"

Bienvenüe shakes his silver head. "All the carriages would be the same, monsieur. All seats priced remarkably low."

Her husband snorts. "I warn you, don't expect my friends to muck in with the hoi polloi down in the reeking catacombs!"

"If it were up to me, I'd make all transit free."

"Free?" Émile laughs at the idea.

Louise's eyes have slid back to her daughter. Jeanne would tell her mother if she felt really ill, surely? Except the girl might well be sicker than she knows. Hard to make sense of lingering sensations. When you're young, growing can hurt, and everything is new and puzzling. You might be the only one in the world to feel this way. The budding self is a sealed compartment, mysterious. Besides, even if Jeanne does suspect these symptoms are serious, what daughter tells her mother everything?

It's true, now Louise is really looking, that Jeanne's as white as paper, shaky, wobbling, a pretty wraith. This is Louise's fault, one way or another; she's failed to protect the treasure she meant to pass down the chain of generations. *How could I have not have felt in my bones that something was very wrong?* Louise has been blinded by love, a veil hanging between her and her daughter. Everyone's noticed Jeanne hasn't been well; Émile asked about it, and Louise said, *A touch of anaemia, so common in girls.* Her stepfather loves Jeanne so much—if she has this awful disease, this *white blood*, it will destroy him.

"I must say, I'm startled by our speed this close to Paris. Sixty-four kilometres an hour." Bienvenüe's studying his watch.

Émile's eyebrows go up. "How can you put a figure on it?"

"Telegraph poles are fifty-five metres apart, so I count them for one minute, then multiply by three point three."

"Well, fast is the way I like it," Émile jokes. "I'd fly to Paris if I could."

He looks to Louise, prompting her to mention the balloon. But she can't summon her wifely forces. He turns back to Bienvenüe and tells him, "I've gone up in a hot-air balloon—though it was rather too slow for me! There's a fellow called

Ader who's tried out a steam-powered flying machine south of Versailles. Claims it carried him two hundred metres!"

Louise notices that Jeanne is swaying a little. Enjoying the dancing movement of the train or dizzy, fading? Louise's little finger hooks onto hers. Her daughter turns and smiles—or summons a smile with effort? But she makes it look easy.

"Tired, my pet?" Louise pats her lap as if Jeanne's much younger than seventeen and they're not sharing a carriage with a male stranger.

Jeanne inches over and puts her head down on her mother's skirts, a cat making herself a nest. Not cold; her face is warm and humid to the touch. (The start of one of those fevers Mademoiselle de Heredia warned about?) Louise cups the round cheek, the firm ear, the light prickle of eyelashes. Even through the terror, such happiness. To be required for such a basic purpose as cushioning; to be the right mother at the right moment with no need for words; to know what comfort your child seeks and have it to give.

———

It's Maurice's bladder that wakes him. He has a crick in his neck from leaning his cheek against the window, and *Around the World in Eighty Days* is splayed on the floor. He didn't know he was going to fall asleep like some toddler or drunk or old man; it's mortifying. Maurice snatches up his book with one hand and rubs his eyes with the other.

He's never seen buildings high enough to loom over the

tracks like this, and so many of them close together. "Are we coming into Dreux?" he asks the lean stranger beside him.

A chuckle. "Outskirts of Paris, boy."

Maurice leaps up, shocked into tears. "I've—" Gulping. "I've missed my stop!"

"Ah, bad luck."

"No, but my father won't know where I am." Back there, sitting in the cart outside the station. Maurice's mind is clouded with panic.

"Keep calm," the nurse tells him. "Tears won't help."

It's her lack of sympathy that steadies Maurice. He nods, sniffing into his sleeve.

"I blame the train," she says darkly. "It puts folks into a stupor—rocks them to sleep."

When he finally finds his parents, could he blame his disastrous lapse on the motion of the train? *If* he finds his parents.

"Just sit tight till Montparnasse," she commands. "Nothing's going to happen to you. What's your name?"

He sniffs again, harder. "Maurice Marland."

"Well, young Marland, when we get in, you can explain yourself to the guard and he'll put you on the next train back to Dreux. It might even be this same train."

His tears start to trickle again. "I don't have another ticket."

"I'll talk to the guard."

For all the nurse's brusqueness, Maurice is grateful.

The lean man goes over to the door and lets the pane down. He opens his coat and holds it as if to . . . oh, he's

216

doing *pipi* out the window, Maurice realises. Nobody says a thing; one or two of the women look away, studiously ignoring the man.

Now Maurice's own need is terribly urgent.

When the man sits down again, he chatters away softly to Maurice. "I was just in Dreux for the day. Well, the half-day. I saw an old castle, and a belfry, and things smashed by a cyclone a few years back."

Maurice rouses himself to answer civilly. "Why didn't you stay longer, monsieur?"

"Oh, I only had half a day off. I work as an alarm clock, waking up my twenty regulars. I tap on their windows with my pole." The man points up to the net overhead, where a telescopic bamboo stick lies. "I use a peashooter for the ones above the second floor."

"Really?" Maurice would love to try that.

"Then at nightfall I fit a little flame on my pole and go around lighting the streetlamps. When they bring the electric to Montparnasse, I don't know what I'll do. Maybe be an angel."

Maurice looks at the clock man, aghast.

A guffaw. "I don't mean die!"

"Oh."

"A guardian angel, it's called. Restaurants pay them to guide drunken customers home."

The word *home* reminds Maurice that he slept through his stop. He says, sobbing, "My father . . ."

"He'll only have to wait a few hours for you—till the evening, at most."

"But he'll . . . my mother . . ." Will it be terror that their little boy has gone and lost himself in the dangerous capital that fills the Marlands, or rage at his childish incompetence, or some mixture of the two?

"Maybe the stationmaster will send a telegram," says the clock man.

Send a telegram to a cart—how would that be done?

But Maurice's bladder is the most pressing problem. He whispers, "I'm very sorry. I really need to . . ."

The clock man catches on right away. "Ah. You can't hold it a little longer?"

He shakes his head. It's taking all his self-control not to wet himself.

They both consider the window in the door. Maurice is just not tall enough. "Unless I lift you up?"

Another shake of the head. Maurice doesn't think he could, under such embarrassing conditions; he might fumble it and leak on the clock man.

"Here." The nurse, who must have heard all this, produces a broad-lipped tin pot. "Take it over by the door."

"But madame—"

"Go on, nobody cares."

Hot-faced, Maurice gives in. Almost pressed against the door, eyes down, trying to shield himself from view, he manages it. The sound goes on and on. Then he succeeds in lowering the glass again, and he tips the hot puddle out into the wind so it splashes the side of the train.

The clock man gives him a nudge and points at a great carousel, brightly painted, bunting aflutter. When Maurice looks closer, he sees that the riders are powering it themselves, by pedalling!

"Ugh." The old priest, rousing himself from his doze. "This city gives me palpitations. There's that monstrosity." He nods at the other window.

Maurice follows his gaze and recognises the extraordinary structure. The postcards didn't prepare him for this—slim and upright and tapering gracefully, like a gigantic dancer made of wire.

"And that's from five or six kilometres away," the priest complains in Maurice's direction. "Wait till you see it up close."

But it's gone already; the city's swallowed it up.

"Or climb it," the clock man suggests.

"You can do that?" Maurice asks, thrilled.

A conspiratorial nod. "It's stairs all the way, with the wind blowing through."

"You can ride up in an elevator, I heard," the brick-brown woman contributes.

The old priest shakes his head. "The arrogance of it, to erect the tallest building in the world in homage not to Our Lord but to science! I marvel it hasn't been levelled yet, like the Tower of Babel."

"It gets struck by lightning all the time," the clock man says mildly, "but the rods carry the power safely down to the ground."

Maurice wants to see Eiffel's monstrosity again, more than anything. To mount those breezy steps into the sky. To feel the lightning sing through the struts.

———

Cécile Langlois is letting out terrible, animal sounds, just like the ones Maman used to make on those worst days of Mado's childhood when hope was lost over and over again in a rush of blood.

The oysterwoman passes Cécile her cider bottle for another swig.

The rain's cleared up, and a big, pale crescent moon hangs in the afternoon sky. A man walking beside the tracks leads a small brown bear on a chain, and Mado thinks she might cry but instead she curses the handler; better to starve than earn your bread by such means. On the left, in the distance, she spots the sprawl of the vast French Society of Munitions and curses that, too, for spewing out hundreds of millions of shotgun cartridges every year. *Soon, so soon, the whole tent will start to rip and come down.*

"Oh, sweet Saviour." Cécile Langlois gasps. "I can't wait."

"Keep your legs together till Montparnasse," the soldier protests from the far end.

"For shame!" The women shout him down.

"How do you imagine you came into the world yourself?" the oysterwoman demands.

Now Vanves Fort rears up, and the train's cutting through

the Firing Zone, that filthy bathtub ring around the capital. In the quarter century since the Prussians marched in and out, the zone's eroded trench and glacis have been kept clear, but housing of a fungal sort has spread across it anyway— peasants squeezed off their farmland, Romani, evicted Parisians squatting in horse stalls, low shanties of tin or tarred cardboard on ground awash with sewage. Mado can see ragpickers bent down, gleaning for rubbish. Graffiti on a wall, as if urging her on: *No gods, no masters.*

A roar. Dripping with sweat, Cécile holds her breath, eyes bulging—

The unmistakable sign that she's bearing down. Mado wishes this whole messy business weren't so familiar so her from her mother's luckless deliveries.

"That's right, Madame Langlois," Madame Baudin encourages, "keep it up. Harder, harder!"

Cécile's heels are up on the bench all at once. Her skirt's spread like a damp valley between the crags of her knees. Her chin presses to her chest as she pushes: "Unhhhh!"

The soldier suddenly shoves his way through the pack. "Air!" He tries to let down the window.

But Madame Baudin shouts, "A cold draught—do you mean to kill her?"

Someone slaps his hand away.

The soldier slings his bag across his body and stumbles over to the door, knocking half a dozen oysters to the floor. He opens it into the blasting wind.

Screeches of protest.

The soldier steps out, grips the rail, and toes his way along the footboard towards the next carriage, leaving their door swinging and the carriage buffeted by wind—

The bowler-hatted man lunges for the handle, grabs it, and slams the door shut.

Blonska grips Cécile's hand. "Be ready for the next one."

Mado can actually hear the wave of pain rising in Cécile's throat, the way the woman sucks in a big breath and holds it while she heaves—

Then lets out a burst of loud air, desperate.

Mado's trying to remember all her reasons. *Property is theft.* (But they're just words right now; they strike no sparks.) She's going to make her great gesture in the name of those who build houses they'll never live in, those who bake bread that they can't afford to feed their children. Mado's striking a blow on behalf of the women going blind over their needles and the girls who can't afford to say no. She's setting off this bomb for her papa, the only one who never lied to her; she's going to make his ignominious life matter.

Never mind reasons now. Mado's vowed to do this terrible, dazzling deed. A purging fire, a red night, a storm, a new dawn.

"Someone has to die."

Everyone turns to stare at the oysterwoman.

"To make room for the new one," she spells out. "Don't you know the saying? *One must die before the next can be born.* Don't worry, Madame Langlois, it shouldn't take long in such a big city."

Mado blinks at the high buildings, the choked streets flickering by. A fur shop with a stuffed tiger, a butcher hanging up a split cow, a fishmonger displaying a tuna taller than a man, an undertaker selling funeral crowns of wired white beads. Like a litter of handbills and flyers, each wall and building is trying to sell something—*Liberator Cycles, Vermouth, Biscuits, Music New and Secondhand, Casino, Egg Mousse, Manicure with Electric Massage.* A chimney sweep's leading his tiny, black-caked boy.

Cécile only sobs.

Is she wondering whether it'll be her who has to die? *But it's all of us,* Mado wants to tell her.

"Urghhhh!"

Not long now, Mado would like to whisper in Cécile's ear. Clocks will stop, down tools, work done.

———

Once you let one yawn out, it starts a family. Léon Mariette can't stop yawning as he hunches over his desk in Front Baggage, hedged in by trunks and valises and portmanteaus. All his waybills are in order, weighted down with a horseshoe. But he always has his journey report to fill in on this last run from Dreux. Léon uncaps the little bottle of ink swinging by its string from a nail. (Never more than half full in case the motion of the train makes it slosh.) He checks that his nib is clean and dips his pen. Index finger marking his place on the preprinted form, he consults the notes in his log and fills in the registration numbers of today's crew and the description, depot, and vehicle number of each piece of rolling stock.

Another huge yawn. Léon dropped off over dinner the other night, and Marie wasn't happy. But it's hardly his fault if he's up half the night fretting over omissions and fudgings in that day's paperwork. Now he adds to the journey report each halt with the time of arrival and departure and how many minutes late, with any possible justifications.

He finds himself brooding over Camp Hill, that junction in Pennsylvania where some forty years ago, two trains met head-on. It turned out all the American companies were running on fifty different regional times. Scores of passengers burnt to death for want of synchronisation, and a guard, not even to blame, poor fellow, topped himself the next day. What slackers like Jean Le Goff don't grasp is that a railway is a system of standardised, interlocking parts—trains, tracks, staff, passengers—and the system runs smoothly only if every part does what it is designed to, down to the millimetre and the second.

Léon still has to add the final details at the very moment of arrival at Montparnasse so he can hand the report over to the waiting clerk for scrutiny. He wipes his watering eyes with both hands, then closes them for just a moment and lays his forehead down on his right wrist. *Gather your forces. Very soon your shift will be done.*

His sleepy mind slips back through a haze of nostalgia to his days in the Zouaves. Those baggy trousers were the most comfortable item of clothing he's ever worn. Very decent fellows he met in the army, for the most part—conscripts from mainland France as well as enlisted Arabs. Always a superior to give orders, so most of the time all the privates had to do was stand guard, which really meant waiting, leaning against a sunbaked wall . . .

Henry Tanner can tell they're in Paris proper by the graceful green cast-iron street furniture: lampposts curled like ferns, public benches, Wallace drinking fountains with their nymphs and dolphins, domed Morris columns covered in posters. "The ones by popular artists never last long," he tells Marcelle de Heredia. (They're back to English, as a concession to him.) "The pal with whom I share a studio pinched us a seven-foot poster of Sarah Bernhardt."

She laughs at that.

Painter and physiologist, American and Frenchwoman, the two of them are swapping tales as if they're catching up after years apart. Marcelle pours out a long story about a pale girl in First Class, a racing-car driver's stepdaughter, who may have a fatal blood disorder, "unless I'm mistaken, which I easily could be, in which case I've set off a land mine under a family's happiness for nothing."

"They're probably not happy," Henry objects, "not if the daughter's ill, and they don't know why, and nothing seems to help."

Marcelle lets out a long sigh. "I dread to think that what made me speak up was my longing to be right. The thrill of knowing—as if I'm the only one in the world with the solution to the puzzle."

Henry wonders whether every scientist, like every artist—like every person who puts in ridiculous hours at work they love—isn't motivated in part by vanity. "You were trying to alert them to a grave danger."

"But to what end?" she asks bitterly. "I've never heard of any cure for leukaemia, so what good is a diagnosis? When you can't avert disaster, perhaps it's better not to see it coming."

"Ignorance is bliss? Really?"

Her mouth twists at Henry's comment. "Well, not bliss, but . . . peace."

"An illusory peace."

Marcelle shrugs. "As all peace is."

She can't possibly share his faith; Henry knows that without asking, and it weighs on his heart. "You're judging yourself too harshly. Because *you'd* no doubt prefer to know the truth about your own health—"

"Of course I would."

"All you did was forget, briefly, that others may prefer not to know. People are so very unalike."

"Yes," she murmurs.

How unalike are Henry Tanner and the lovely Marcelle de Heredia, for instance; so many ways they're mismatched.

He wants, needs, to tell her another story. "My mother's mother, a Virginian slave"—the word comes out without the usual sting of mortification—"she had eleven children. One by one, over the years, she put them into an oxcart going north so they could grow up free, without her."

Marcelle's face puckers with what looks like pain. Then it smoothens out. "And now her grandson rides the Paris Express."

Disconcerted, Tanner imagines his forebears in the fields straightening up to watch him rush by on a fierce, inexhaustible machine. The very puff of the engine seems to say, *Pourquoi pas?* Why not, why the heck not?

"We are two free persons of colour riding on a train, are we not?" Marcelle asks. "And no one can stop us from riding this train."

"No. I mean yes, we are."

"And on the horizon, little more than four years away, is the twentieth century. What a ring that has to it."

Henry smiles back at her. How crass would it be to ask where her father lives with a view to calling on the two of them?

⊢————⊣

In John's carriage, Annah Lamor stands up to powder her face at the mirror as unashamedly as if she's in her own room. She flicks a few smuts off her nose, then puts her little puff in its jar and pushes her way to the window, her orange skirt spilling over many pairs of knees. Her broad nose is pressed to the glass when a crow swoops by.

The Dubliner watches. Her plumage reminds him of

Hermes, messenger of the gods, with his winged feet. Now, that would be the best way to travel—simply put your sandals on and fly . . .

After four o'clock today, I won't see you again, he tells her silently. Unless he sought out her morbid Cabaret of Nothingness. Not that a fellow without a spare franc would be any use to Annah Lamor. Sometimes John thinks that women are all that make him feel alive, and he'll never get to touch one.

The sudden darkness of a tunnel, fogged with the train's smoke and steam.

Now at last the Express is surging into John's own ramshackle *quartier*, Montparnasse. Six-floor rooming houses press close to the track. This transplanted Irishman takes an odd pride in the fact that the little tables outside the cafés are full, even on a crisp October day. An auction house is advertising a Grand Sale of Fancy Feathers. John spots, painted on a wall, the familiar coat of arms of Paris: a little boat with the motto *Fluctuat nec mergitur*—"Tossed but not sunk."

Annah's hoot startles him. She jerks her thumb at a passing street. "Rue Vercingétorix."

It sounds like one of Julius Caesar's campaigns.

"I keep house for that painter," she explains. "Two rooms, top of number six."

"You live at number six?" John's foolishly disappointed that this chimerical creature is, well, spoken for.

A cluck of her tongue. "Not *now*. Years back. Gauguin."

"Oh, yes, this painter, you said."

"Yellow walls, axes, boomerangs."

"Axes and boomerangs?" John echoes, bewildered.

"Two rooms, so full of stuff, no space to move! Always he puts me in his pictures with no clothes," Annah complains.

Synge grits his teeth at the image. A Frenchman using this uprooted child as maid, nude model, and mistress.

"His friends come to drink and smoke and take photographs. I don't mind photographs," Annah says, "except no smiling."

"You weren't smiling?"

"I never smile in pictures. It's stupid." Her eyes are hazy with reminiscence. "In Brittany where they throw stones—"

"This Gauguin brought you to Brittany?" John asks. "The time they called you a witch?"

A nod. "He sends me back here to *tidy up*, so, ha! I sell it all."

"You sold the painter's stuff while he was out of town?"

"Axes, boomerangs, chairs, rugs, even the bed. Rooms look better. Bigger." Annah's lit up with pleasure at the memory. "I can't sell his pictures, though."

"No?"

"Nobody will pay a sou for his stupid pictures."

And John's laughing too at the idea of this horrible painter opening the door and finding nothing left, no little brown girl, no bed, no weapons, nothing interrupting the gleaming expanse but his own canvases staring back at him.

"That song with the railwaymen dancing," Max Jacob says without warning, his eyes on the track that runs alongside this one, "I have it stuck in my head."

"Hmm," says his friend. "I'm afraid I can't think of the one—"

"You know it, Kiouaup! That operetta of Offenbach's set at Montparnasse Station? The foreigners burst in—" Max breaks into song in a startlingly sonorous voice:

> *We're hitting Paris en masse,*
> *Rushing into town*
> *To have a blast—*
> *Make room for us!*

"I like that," says John. Thinking that, yes, that's why he and all these restless souls have fetched up in Montparnasse, out of all the villages that fit together like puzzle pieces to make up Paris. This neighbourhood harbours them, entertains them, lets them do what they like. *Makes room for us.*

"The head's out!" Blonska's kneeling in a gaudy puddle between Cécile Langlois's thighs, considering a protruding fair haired crown.

Most of the other passengers are gasping and groaning as if the pain is their own. This is an impossible sight if you've never seen it before—a tiny person half out of another person, on the very cusp of separation. One becomes two, the original magic trick.

Blonska turns up the hem of her skirt—no, her blouse is cleaner, so she yanks it out of her waistband and swabs the tiny, flat nose. The eyes mere slits. She can't tell yet whether it's alive.

Her gaze slides back to the lunch bucket on Mado's lap as it has over and over since Dreux. The agony of this suspense. How to carry on minute by minute when you don't know how long you've got.

Madame Baudin is holding Cécile up, urging her on. "One more push, *ma chère*."

Nobody says a word while the blonde heaves. "Unhhhhh!"

Nothing happens except that this strange, scarlet berry with its slick of ermine rotates a little. The miniature nostrils flare. Not dead, then.

What Blonska reads on that small face is not so much innocence as a stoic disenchantment, a readiness despite everything.

Cécile lets out a wail of lamentation. She pushes again, hard, vainly.

Half-born and mother, locked together. Infant trapped in the vise of mother's bone; mother pinned and tortured by her own infant. Miraculous creation, mutual destruction. Nature's best idea and her worst. It comes to Blonska with a cold clarity: *The shoulder's stuck.*

Just then Mado throws her a sidelong glance.

It's enough for Blonska to look back and hook her gaze. She extemporizes crazily: "Mademoiselle Pelletier!" Barking the name. "Lend a hand, won't you, just for a minute?"

The girl's eyes narrow.

"It's the shoulder, it's jammed."

A deafening silence.

"I know you know about these things! Won't you have some compassion?" Blonska pleads.

Will Mado say *Go to hell?* Will she burst out laughing and set off her bomb?

She gets to her feet, swaying stiffly with the motion of the train. She bends to set down the lunch bucket. As the handle peels away from her fingers, the thing nearly tips over and Blonska's pulse stops—

But Mado snatches at it and steadies it. Shoves the lunch bucket into the corner of the carriage, under her bench.

"Oh, never mind your blasted lunch," Madame Baudin says, incredulous.

Blonska has Cécile's stockinged shins in her hands and she's shoving the woman's knees upwards and outwards. "Sorry, sorry, I'm just trying to widen—"

The next pain comes in like a bear. Cécile shrieks and strains, her soles to the sky like some parody of a whore. Are they all about to see a woman ripped in two?

"Brandy," Mado demands.

"She's had most of my cider already," the oysterwoman mutters.

"Absinthe, then. Any bloody spirit at all."

Someone passes a bottle from the back; eau de vie, it looks like to Blonska. Mado sloshes the brandy over her hands, rubbing them hard. Then upends the bottle over Cécile's purplish, bulging parts—

Making her howl again.

"Hold her," Mado orders, and Blonska and Madame Baudin tighten their grip as Mado approaches with a wet, shaking hand that's marked with the dark line of the handle she's been gripping all day. Remorseless, she pushes two fingers into the awful line between flesh lip and infant neck, between half-born and mother, until her fingers disappear. Mado closes her eyes. Blonska wonders how the girl can possibly find what she's fishing around for in all that pressure and heat.

A minute rubbery arm flips out beside the tiny head as if waving.

———

Still full steam ahead, which is troubling Victor—when's Guillaume going to start slowing down? Can it really be worth the risk of speeding into the city just to make up a minute or so?

It's a straight slope down to Montparnasse Station, where they'll draw into the leftmost platform on the upper level. Victor's legs will be shaking by the time he gets down. He lets himself look forward to journey's end—the finish line of this nerve-racking race. A bucket of warm water for washing himself, a hot dinner. He wonders what Joséphine will have made him tonight. She's a good woman; he hasn't a word to say against her. She just doesn't know him the way his mate does.

Here's rue de la Procession, and Guillaume finally gives the nod. With relief, Victor shoves the air brake's brass handle all the way open.

No response.

233

He stares at the lever in shock. So does Guillaume. The whites of his eyes; a barked question that's swept away by the smoky wind.

The Westinghouse system can't fail. Victor swivels the handle back, then tries again, more violently. Nothing. Which is impossible. *"Putain!"*

Guillaume almost shoves Victor aside and yanks at the air brake. Then does it again. A third time.

Victor interrogates himself. Could they have depleted the air pressure in the reservoirs, not leaving enough time for a full recharge? No; since Granville they've barely tapped on the brake. Has the pressure cylinder cracked? Could a ball joint have popped and broken the tube's link to the rest of the train? An angle cock left closed by accident? Even sabotage?

But the air brake's designed to work by default, slamming into force as soon as anything cuts the connection.

Or is the answer a simpler one—has Guillaume applied it so very late at such high speed that the air brake's just no match for the massive momentum of Engine 721? He dashes back to the tender, where the hand brake is.

"Reverse steam?" Victor roars. Not that it's a question, really, but he's never in all these years told his driver what to do. Not till this moment, thundering past the points at rue du Château with only, what, eight hundred metres to go, and his mind moving as sluggishly as honey. A plea this time: "Reverse steam!"

Has Guillaume even heard him? The driver seizes the

metal cross that operates the screw of the hand brake and turns it all the way around, three times—not that those iron clamps chewing on the wheels will be able to do much except produce an awful screeching.

Victor can't wait. He grabs the reversing wheel, opens every steam cock to push the pistons backwards. The train skids past a signal that has its arm in the horizontal position and its lamp flaring furiously behind its red lens. He can hear the operator rapidly banging his gong to sound the alarm, but still the terrible convoy moves on. *Air, friction, steam—* they've tried everything but nothing's working fast enough to stop this behemoth before the buffers.

Guillaume's yanking the steam whistle now, two short, jerky blasts to tell Léon and Jean to slam on their own brakes. Victor belatedly remembers that the driver should have whistled to the guards when the air brake first failed. But you can't do everything at once when everything needs doing and there's no time . . . *What else, what else?* He snatches at all four levers of the sandbox to release sand down the hoses in front of the wheels to see if a bit of grit will help, though if a train's going too fast, sand can actually make matters worse by letting the wheels grip the rails more tightly, but he has to try something, doesn't he, he cannot just stand here pop-eyed less than five hundred metres from the hard oak buffers lying in wait at the end of the line.

Now even the ladies in the Gévelot party notice what's been troubling Jules-Félix. "I've never known a train to whiz through town so," Emma says uneasily.

"I suppose they're trying to get us there on time"—Aimée checks her little watch on its chain—"or not so *very* late."

Jules-Félix catches sight of a couple of railwaymen on a platform, their arms in the air as if hailing a conqueror—perhaps mockingly? No, waving in horror. Under his breath, in the comte de Lévis-Mirepoix's direction: "I don't believe we can stop."

Aimée catches that. "What do you mean? How can we not stop?"

"We're going to crash?" Emma almost whispers it, as if saying the words aloud will make it so. She's seized her friend's hand.

Not her husband's; Jules-Félix notices that. Of course, he's not sitting beside her as Aimée is. He's on his feet, all at once ready for action, as if there were something he could do—he, one of more than a hundred helpless little ants in this speeding machine. The comte is also standing, staring furiously out the window. Jules-Félix supposes men (aristos and bourgeoisie and workingmen too) have been brought up to do this in situations of danger: to make themselves taller and mill around, however foolishly.

He's pretty certain there's no escape at this point. "Lift your feet," he barks at the ladies. "When we hit, the train will shut up like a telescope, see?" Jules-Félix mashes his fists together. Matter will condense, and so will time. The ladies are not moving. "These benches will sever your legs."

"Darling," Emma says reproachfully.

"Get up!"

The two friends leap onto the padded banquette, on their knees, still holding hands. Should Jules-Félix try to interpose his body between them and harm? As if his stout frame could be anything but a crushing weight when the train hits. *No, stay by the door.* He'll have some slim chance of being of use in the aftermath if the impact doesn't take his own legs.

His bowels are a little loose from terror.

What hits him is the unfairness: *Why me?* Which is absurd, he realises, even as the train shakes and roars. Really, the odd thing is that Jules-Félix Gévelot, famed across the world (and especially on the soaked battlefields of America) for being what the plainspoken might call a dealer in death, hasn't come within a whisker of it till now. Like the parasitical aristocrat at his side, Jules-Félix has done no military service, having been too busy as a captain of industry since the age of eighteen. He supposes he could be said to have killed untold numbers for France, albeit at several removes; does that count?

Another question: Will he prove a coward when it comes to it? *A dummy, a dud, a squib, an utter blank?* Faces in the window flit by. This is the final station, the end of the line.

Emma and Aimée are clinging to the baggage nets overhead so they won't topple off the banquette; they dangle like apes. They have their faces pressed together, whispering—what? Prayers, pleas, vows?

Jules-Félix suddenly registers something: He lost his wife to this woman years ago. There are forms of betrayal so discreet that no one thinks to gossip about them; invisible adulteries.

And, really, has he any right to complain? This complicated marriage has had three people in it, and perhaps that's been the secret of its success; he's been allowed to immerse himself in work. So how fitting that all three of the Gévelot household are about to come to their end together.

Time, just a little more time!

But it was never his to hold, to hide from the great thief, death. It's all borrowed, Jules-Félix realises, every second of it.

———

In the very front passenger carriage, Alice Guy and her boss stare out opposite windows. This seems much too fast for a train to approach the terminus; however are they going to stop in time? Alice sees a railwayman by the track, wild-eyed—then gone already. The next man flaps both hands overhead as if to tell her something. The Express is a comet shooting past.

Gaumont's saying something but she's not listening. She lifts the moving-picture camera and sets it on the little table with a thump, its lens almost touching the window. Not a view of a train coming into a station, but the world as seen by someone on a train, or even the train's own point of view.

A bewildering succession of images, perhaps nothing but a blur, a waste of ten seconds of film, but worth a try, no? Everything's worth trying once, especially if the train's about to crash, and most especially if Alice Guy, twenty-two, has only a matter of seconds left.

She snatches the cap off the lens and starts to crank the handle as if her life depends on it.

⊢――――⊣

At the very back of the train, Jean Le Goff lets out a yowl of frustration. What's Mariette up to in his little birdcage in Front Baggage? But the senior guard's not authorised, no more than Jean is, to do a thing unless and until the driver sounds the alarm. What the hell are the rollers playing at up there?

Jean eyes his leather-covered wooden crank. It's as much as his job's worth for a junior guard to slam on a rear air brake without permission. Then again, what's the worst it could do—slow the train down? Which could only be a good thing as they skid towards the buffers.

Hang on, though. If Jean halts his end but the engine, tender, and ten carriages keep moving forward, will it break the coupling apart and derail the whole kit and caboodle in the middle of the crowded city; would it be like scissoring through a taut string? Chill sweat in the small of Jean's back. If only he'd applied himself harder to his books during training or ever looked at them in the years since . . . if only he weren't a careless *connard* who may be about to cause mass carnage because of his ignorance of the laws of physics . . .

Pellerin's steam whistle, at last—two rapid blares, the emergency alarm.

Jean hurls himself on the air brake and shoves the handle to the right to open the valve all the way. For good measure, he seizes the metal cross of the hand brake and turns the screw twice to tighten the clamps' grip on the wheels. A metallic scream below him, a terrible pressure and drag, but he can't tell whether he's doing anything to slow this runaway train . . .

God save us. His head jerks briefly to the left as they screech past his lodgings on rue de Vouillé. Nothing he can do now but cling to the brake to keep the pressure up and hope against hope that—

The form Léon Mariette's filling in is getting longer; it stretches and sags. Impossibly long now, dangling and curling like a hank of wool and beginning to tangle itself into knots. He fights with the clinging fibres. He slashes with his pen. If he can only climb up to the top of the snagged vines, leap lightly and fly free . . . but an elephant's trumpet startles him. Birds scatter and scream. Which way is the danger? Louder, a short, repeated, stabbing sound; he can't think, can't move, can't—

Léon wakes blinking, bewildered, to find his face glued to the crumpled ledger. He rips it away and only then realises he must have dropped off for a moment, for a minute maybe. The next thing he registers is that the awful sounds in his dream can only have been the emergency alarm.

He stumbles away from his desk; his chair drops with a clatter. The window shows Montparnasse coming up so fast, Léon grasps that the Express is about to smash. Pellerin's alarm is an order to the guards to apply the brake, but which one, the air brake here on the floor of the van or the hand brake above? The air brake's more powerful, unless the Westinghouse system's somehow failed, which it must have done if the rollers haven't managed to stop the train yet, so Léon throws himself up the ladder to his birdcage and claws at the cross of the hand brake, cranking it one full rotation before—

4:00 p.m.
ARRIVE PARIS-
MONTPARNASSE

Every body perseveres in its state of rest, or of uniform
motion in a right line, unless it is compelled to
change that state by forces impressed thereon.

ISAAC NEWTON,
PRINCIPIA (1687)

Paris-Montparnasse Station is a neoclassical temple of
stone, steel, and glass, a hive buzzing with hustle and
bustle. The four tracks are stacked two by two to take up less
space in this crowded neighbourhood, and the Express from
Granville always comes in on the upper level, high above Place
de Rennes. Up there, the platform clocks are showing 4:00
p.m. Streams of people are mingling, impatient to meet the
Express. The train cleaners set down their brimming galvan-
ised buckets and lean on their mops, their skirts festooned

with wash leathers. Stalls peddle umbrellas, shoelaces, toys, sweets, books. On a wheeled stove, a Breton woman is frying crepes, a familiar fragrance to hook the homesick.

Whatever's about to befall Engine 721, for once in her long career she will be more than just a means of transportation. Headline news on every front page. The eyes of the world—those burning spotlights—are about to turn on her at last.

As the screaming train skids into the station, slowing, slowing, but not fast enough, Guillaume braces the reversing wheel with his right hand and clutches the rod with his left, sounding the whistle. On the platform to his right, he glimpses station staff huddling behind a desk. He remembers a rule, or is it only a proverb? *The captain always goes down with his ship.* But Victor, poor sooty Victor at his left—the man whose scarred body Guillaume knows every inch of from their days on the footplate as well as their nights in the boardinghouse, cots jammed together, nights of embraces the two of them never mention to a soul, not even each other—

"Jump!" Guillaume roars.

No answer from his dear mate, who's staring out the left side, gripping the handrail.

All Guillaume can do is hold on, while—

In the Place de Rennes below, carriages and cabs wait by the tram terminus, which is usually crammed with multiple vehicles, but right now there's only one tram, bound for the Arc de Triomphe, with a few dozen passengers waiting bundled up on its two decks. Pacing up and down beside her stack of newspapers, Marie Haguillard winds her black shawl around her neck against the chill and looks up at the station, where the roof ridge rises into a double peak, like joined eyebrows over the two great glass half-moons. A clock is set like a forehead jewel between these lunette windows, and it shows five minutes past four.

The men in Marie's family are all carpenters; her brother Joseph's already started teaching one of her boys to handle tools (the bigger one, not the little one, who's all thumbs). But at thirty-eight, Marie will turn her hand to anything to earn her bread, so she's both seamstress and newspaper seller; she starts sewing at first light, then stands in for her man, Jules, while he goes to collect the evening editions (which takes two hours, and he comes back reeking of marc). Marie knows not to expect too much of Jules, her husband *in the hay*, as they say, who has a legal wife already.

An oddly quiet October afternoon. Not that Paris is ever quite still—there's always something, the hooves of passing cavalry, or bicycle bells, or the deeper clanging of a distant fire engine.

The sharp breeze flaps the edges of Marie's stack of five-centime dailies, so she weighs it down with a loose cobble half the size of her head. She and Jules stock the *Little Parisian*, and the *Radical*, and the *Little Journal*—when she gets a spare minute, Marie likes to look at the engravings and horoscopes in that one. They always have a few copies of *Le Figaro*—at fifteen centimes, strictly for the bourgeoisie who delude themselves it's written three times better than the others—and the *Gaul*, for the last few snooty monarchists in Montparnasse. Yellow journalism, to be read on the fly today and used for wiping arses tomorrow. For customers on the tram's lower deck, Marie hands the papers in the window, but for the upper floor, she has to use a bamboo pole with a mug lashed to the top for them to drop the coins in.

It's a dull news day; Marie can tell from the small size of the headline type. "'Visit of King of Portugal,'" she bawls out, doing her best. "'Death of Monsieur Bonghi.'" Whoever that is. *Le Figaro* has not a single headline worth shouting out today; "Architecture Competition" would actually put customers off. Ooh, here's a juicy one from the *Little Journal*; Marie roars gothically, "'Disappearance of Young Girls'!"

No, nobody will take a paper off her hands. Killing time, Marie pulls out her knitting to put new toes and heels into a pair of Gaston's socks; the boy's feet are as leathery as a soldier's.

———

A young photographer's pedalling down rue de Rennes from the office of Lévy, the postcard publishers, to their print workshop, the address from which their pictures wing around the world. The firm's already built up a collection of thirty thousand images—the Pyramids, the Alhambra, the Statue of Liberty—but they're always looking for more, so this young man lives in hope that the Lévys might choose an eye-catching photograph of his. You never know, do you? Mounted on his handlebars by two lugs, in case there's only time for a snapshot, is his tarnished silver-plated Photosphère with its hemispherical bulge and lens that protrudes like a nipple.

The station's sending up a dragon's breath darkening the air, which bewilders Marie Haguillard as she stands in the square below. The horses lashed to the nearby tram are twitchy; all at once, their heads snap up in unison and they're off, yanking the tram away on its track set into the cobblestones, passengers hanging on to their seats. The cabs, too, and the private carriages—they scatter in different directions like dust because all the horses in the square are bolting away from the tram terminus. Animals act without thinking, whereas people wait for explanations. Marie stands looking up at the façade, sore feet frozen to the ground. What's this rumbling? Why is she blinking instead of running? (But what should she run from, and which way?)

On the station's upper level, as the Express grinds along the too-horribly-short platform, Guillaume knows he can't save his train from the collision. And suddenly he finds himself balking at the prospect of sacrificing himself and his beloved mate. Why be loyal to the Company when it uses its men as raw material?

He shrieks: "Jump!"

But Victor shows no sign of hearing him. A pile of mail-bags is coming up on Guillaume's right, and—

His legs choose for him. He launches himself into space.

The platform comes up to punish him. He hits the bags belly-down and hard, all the breath smashed out of him, and keeps going, rolling across the stone floor like a gambler's die. He can't get purchase and doesn't stop till he drops onto the next track over.

⊢————⊣

Like a knife turning the world to butter, Engine 721 bursts through the wooden buffers.

Her stoker, Victor Garnier, gripping the rail beside his controls like Samson did the temple columns, is thrown clear of the footplate; he flies free, crashes into the awning of the customs booth, and lands in a tangle of limbs. But Engine 721 somehow carries on, her momentum thrusting her through the stonework, sparks cascading through billows of steam and smoke as she mounts the platform and scrapes across thirty metres of marble concourse to pierce the station's front wall.

⊢————⊣

Marie Haguillard stands in the square like her pillar of papers until she sees it; in fact. she's the only one in the world to see it, the Express bursting out of the lunette on the right like a dagger out of an eye—the pointed tip of the engine piercing stone façade and concrete balustrade as if it were paper. Marie is the sole witness, history's honoured guest, for half a second, before the engine plunges and the air turns to rock and falls—

Erasing her.

4:01 p.m.

---

*All that happened in
the space of a second.*

MONTPARNASSE STATIONMASTER,
"A SHATTERED STATION,"
GIL BLAS (OCTOBER 24, 1895)

Towards the back of the train, the impact's felt only as a shaking, but that's enough to tip the lunch bucket onto its side.

Crouched between Cécile's legs, gripping the tiny arm and head in her bloody hands, Mado watches her bomb roll away. Her whole self roars out *NO*—

The lunch bucket lodges lightly against the foot of Madame Baudin, who reaches down without looking and stands it up again.

The train seems to have stopped. Nothing's moving. Except Cécile's baby, shooting out almost too fast for Mado to catch in her skirt.

Up in his birdcage at the front, Léon finds he's . . . stunned, winded that's all. No sign of injury; elbows only a little jarred from bracing himself. He blinks cinders out of his lashes. His Front Baggage van has somehow stuck on the crumbled remains of the station's balcony like a piece of bread between a giant's teeth.

Below him, the tender (spilling coal) and the engine dangle monstrously. Black and white vapours belch, puff, and swirl; embers dot the air with fire. The muffled jerk of the rods, the pulse of the twin pistons still pumping.

The poor rollers! Are Pellerin and Garnier crushed on their footplate underneath him or trapped and burning? Léon turns around and cranes his neck for a view of the rest of the train behind him. The Post Van, the eight passenger carriages, and Rear Baggage are all parked tidily on the gored concourse underneath a clock stopped at exactly four. How bizarre; what astonishing luck.

Front Baggage is poised on the very rim of the gaping hole in the façade and balcony; he realises it could lurch forward at any moment, following engine and tender like slithering links in a chain. And pulling the rest of the train down with it. He has to get out.

Léon's right-hand door is blocked by girders. He tries the left. It opens onto rubble. Will it give way underfoot? Will the whole front of the station cave in?

No choice. Léon lets himself drop. He lands well on a slab

but stumbles sideways, and that's when a rusty piece of metal sticks him in the thigh.

⊢━━━━━┥

In Second Class, at the head of the passenger carriages, Alice (dishevelled, nursing one shoulder) is on her feet, tucking her shirtwaist back into her skirt. Outraged. The very idea that she might have died today in a tangle of metal and blue corduroy upholstery having done precisely *nothing* with her time on this earth—

"Come on." Arms full of their luggage, Gaumont's shepherding her out.

But Alice turns back, almost colliding with him, and retrieves Demenÿ's heavy camera from the corner. "You'll let me borrow this." Not asking, but telling.

"What?" Gaumont's head to one side, as if reckoning whether she's concussed.

"Promise!"

"Whatever you like—take the blasted camera!"

Alice presses it to her, its capped lens digging into her ribs, and rushes to the door.

⊢━━━━━┥

In the next carriage, Marcelle feels her blood tingling like sugar in her veins as she rubs her bruised face. She grabs her typewriter case with one hand and with the other accepts the hand that Henry's holding out. Warmth surges between their bare fingers.

He helps her down the steps to the platform. He's limping a little.

Two guards rush up, demand to know whether the lady's hurt.

At once Marcelle releases his hand. "No, but this gentleman seems to have sprained his ankle."

Awkwardness slides its screen between them. Marcelle's parents knew she was on her way in from Granville today; the minute they hear about a crash, they'll be worried sick. "Thank you, Mr. Tanner, and good day," she says in English, and hurries off.

Levassor and Bienvenüe have their heads out the window of Front First, checking whether anything's on fire. "All I felt was one hard bump, a skid, and then another," Bienvenüe marvels.

Louise has made herself into a cage around her daughter. She's saying to death, *Not yet, not yet.*

"Quick march." Her husband is holding out a hand for each of them.

"Don't forget Ouah-Ouah!" Jeanne dives to grab the cocker spaniel.

Albert deposits his little grandson carefully on the platform beside the Christophle carriage and leaps back up the steps. "Anna?" Will his wife be in a state of absolute hysteria?

When he pulls back the heavy drape, she's sitting up,

holding her greyhound to her chest. Her voice oddly steady: "We're all right."

Albert lifts woman and dog, and they feel as light as an armful of hay.

———

In Rear First, the Gévelots and the comte de Lévis-Mirepoix gape at each other.

"Probably anarchists," Jules-Félix says as soothingly as he can.

They all nod.

Jules-Félix is expecting to feel relief, even euphoria, at having survived. But no, only a sort of suspension, as if the sword's still dangling overhead. He'll always know, now, how close he came. He feels every one of his sixty-nine years.

"Well," Emma murmurs, "Cook had better send up a nice dinner tonight, is all I can say."

———

In Front Third, the baby—ah, another wretched female—lies in Mado's lap in a rusty puddle. Shockingly large for a creature that not a minute ago was part and parcel of her sobbing mother. Pale and limp, hair almost translucently fair.

Silent, unmoving. After all that, is the new Langlois not going to make it, worn out before her story even starts?

"Come on!" Mado shouts at her. She pulls up her stained skirt and scrubs the infant's sticky back with it. "Come on!"

A sound goes up, the thinnest of cries.

Cécile mutters something exhausted and reaches out a hand.

Mado dumps the newborn on the mother's bodice. Cécile half laughs. Mado snatches a chequered cloth off somebody's basket, lays it over the baby's back, and keeps rubbing. Weeping as she works.

⊢────────┤

In the next carriage back, John and the other students are trying to puzzle out how the train ripped right through the end of the track and somehow skated across the concourse.

The maid and manservant in matching livery who got on at Briouze have cut lips rouged with blood. They must have been sitting so close that their faces bumped together—or did they kiss when it seemed as if it might be their last moment on earth? Covertly John watches the maid pull out a handkerchief and wipe her lover's face tenderly before her own.

Why didn't he think to kiss Annah just before the crash? Two of her plumes dangle askew now, broken. Her monkey gibbers.

Max pulls his head back in. "The engine seems to be *gone*."

Annah lets out a flabbergasted cackle, as if she's seen it all now.

Monsieur Dois laughs too as he wrestles with the door. He has to kick it twice before it pops open, and they all spill out.

They squint at the fuming debris of the distant crash site, where the parcel and baggage vans appear to be perched ...

in the clouds? Then they're all staggering about, weak with merriment.

In the rearmost passenger carriage, the old priest is on his knees, arms high, giving thanks in Latin.

"Well, that's the last train I'm ever setting foot in." The nurse's tone is triumphant. She has the little girl on her hip, and she holds out her other hand to Maurice. "Come along."

Grateful, he takes it.

On the platform, Victor's got himself up onto his knees. Battered all over, left thumb twisted so badly, he doesn't know if he'll ever get it straight. "Guillaume!" He lurches upright. The mortification of having let slip the rail and allowed himself to be flung off his engine. He abandoned his post in extremis; worst of all, he abandoned his mate. "Guillaume!" Grief is heading Victor's way, unbearable loss, because the man he loves must be lying torn apart under these murderous wheels.

Just the other side of the train, on the empty track, Guillaume's still stretched out stunned. Nobody's yet noticed him down there in the shadows. He doesn't hear his stoker calling his name. He lies still as if dead, because he should be, but his heart's jangling like the last coin in a tin. Tears stick his face to the wooden sleeper. Guillaume wonders what's broken; he deserves whatever he gets. To have leapt off before the collision like a coward and left the man he loves to be torn apart—

―――――――

Jean, at the very back, jumps down onto the platform without a scratch on him. The junior guard breaks into a run, pushing against the tide of passengers fleeing from the front wall, where the Express seems to disappear into a broken sky. He has to find out what's happened to his crew.

―――――――

The white-blond newborn is slumped on the dome of her mother's belly. Blonska's cut the cord with her sewing scissors and tied it with threads pulled from her sleeve. The other women have donated various bits of cloth for swaddling, and a few coins.

"Never wash her head, it'll make her an idiot," the oysterwoman advises Cécile.

"You're the idiot," Madame Baudin tells the oysterwoman.

Mado's wiping her face hard, scrubbing away the wet. Her grand plan, gone to pot. She won't be setting off any bomb today.

What's shaming her most is the realisation that her tears aren't for baby or mother or any of the fellow passengers she was fully intending to slaughter. They're for herself. Mado can taste the childish disappointment, the vanity in her grief. It seems she wanted glory, the same martyr's crown as handsome

Émile Henry on the guillotine, and she was willing to build a pyre of human beings to win it. She sickens herself.

Mado puts her satchel strap over her shoulder and picks up her heavy lunch bucket. When Blonska glances up from the baby, Mado meets her eyes, but only for a moment.

She shoves open the door and goes down the steps, holding the device carefully away from her legs. She strides down the platform until she spots a rubbish bin. She stands over it, hunching so no one can see her hands fumble to unscrew the lunch bucket's lid. She lifts out the two tiny, wadded vials of acid and tucks them, still upright, into her breast pocket. She'll trickle them into the first drain she finds to mingle silently with the rest of the Paris shit. She upends the metal bucket and lets its mingled grits (charcoal, saltpetre, sugar, match heads) spill into the bin, then finds a rag in her pocket, wipes it out, and sets the thing down beside the bin with a clatter.

Mado pushes through the excited crowd. A bewildered station boy at the gate asks for her ticket, and she almost laughs but she keeps walking, down the stairs and past the gathering gawkers.

Out onto Place de Rennes, where she stops to stare at the gigantic, almost upright locomotive with its nose buried in the ground.

The birth, the train crash, all this high drama, and none of her doing—is the universe mocking Mado, reminding her that she's only an infinitesimally tiny piece of the puzzle? *No accidents.* She wonders whether her first twenty-one years were always leading here. Are we borne along, never knowing who we'll be or what we'll do any more than we know where the track will turn or when it'll come to a stop?

Well. Still a filthy world, but Mado seems to have chosen a side; she's going to have to leave it a little cleaner than she found it. She turns, her sturdy legs bearing her away.

<hr>

The young photographer stands blinking, the air still thick with dust.

A groaning of metal. The great black engine lolls impossibly, balancing on its nose in a puddle of coal, stone, glass, and splintered planks. Above it, the emptied tender, and behind, the baggage van, garlanded with buckled metal and cocked at an angle on the shattered rim of the balcony. A sight as comical as it's apocalyptic, something out of a bad dream, as if Montparnasse Station has vomited out a train.

Urgency grips the photographer; he *must* be the first to capture this. He nudges his bike westwards around the disaster zone, hunting for a composition to give order to this magnificent chaos. It's all too messy, foreground cluttered with gawkers. He nips around a lamppost and moves in closer, till he feels the heat of the dying monster and tastes iron like blood. *Better.* He'll cut out the clock with its little hand stuck at 4:05 because what his photograph's going to capture is an instant out of time. A picture of speed, but frozen. A train unmoving, without driver or passengers, as if shot down from heaven: *deus ex machina.*

Needing his hands free, the young man straddles his bike and clamps it between his legs. He squints down at the Photosphère's tiny viewfinder and takes a breath to steady himself. He moves the bellows like a silent concertina to focus the lens and goes in even tighter.

Putain! Inching into the top left, along the station roof, a pair of little intruders, opaque in the dust cloud. Two station crewmen, flat caps, hands in pockets, peering from the parapet as if such wonders are part of the working day. One of them's pointing down, because who could look at anything else?

No, the photographer can see now that they're gesturing past the engine at the debris outside his frame. He looks up, eyes watering. Only a few metres from him, two other workmen are tugging at a great lump of rubble in a welter of torn papers. The black of some rag—

No, black and red. The scarlet that can only be blood. Something with shoes. The black is a shawl, and the shoes are on feet.

The photographer's gorge is rising.

They don't falter, these men; how can they not balk at this? A third runs up with—*no, no, no.* A bucket. All three are crouching and scooping it, the red, *her,* what's left of this anonymous woman, the wearer of those shoes, that shawl, scraping her into the bucket.

The young man leans away from his camera and retches, but nothing comes out. How could he not have spotted her with his trained eye, the woman mangled by the fallen stones, crushed like a grape?

But he still needs his photograph. He checks his camera; it's aimed past the horror. He'll allow the victim some privacy. Or, put another way, he'll leave her out of the picture. He'll simplify, paring down this complicated story to a clean, absurd image of catastrophe, one that will live for the ages. He has the glass plate ready; he thrusts it into the back and fingers the spring-loaded lever that will open the shutter for one-fifth of a second. He takes the shot.

Author's Note

As train crashes went, technically the Montparnasse Derailment of October 22, 1895, was a minor one. The first reaction of several witnesses in and around the railway station was that it had to be yet another anarchist terror attack. (Long before the twenty-first century, residents of big cities had learned to live with this sort of threat.) Once the derailment was determined to be an accident of some sort, it didn't even merit a mention in that year's *Revue générale des chemins de fer* (*General Railways Review*).

However, at the time it received blanket coverage in French newspapers and abroad, accompanied by hand-drawn illustrations based on a dozen or so different photographs taken in the aftermath. What seems to be the first of those photos (see above), showing two workmen on the roof while the air was still filled with dust and smoke, is usually attributed to the studio Lévy Fils et Cie, but the photographer is unknown.

None of the passengers or crew on the Express from Granville were killed or seriously injured, and the staff and members of the public in Paris-Montparnasse Station were similarly lucky. The sole victim was the newspaper seller **Marie Haguillard** (sometimes written as Aguilard, Aguillard, Aiguillard, Aquilard, Aguélard, or Gillart; 1857–1895).

Marie, her sons Gaston Robert and Julien (nine and six at the time), and her brother Joseph lived ten minutes away at 1 rue Guilleminot with a forty-two-year-old costermonger, Jules Sansiquet (sometimes spelled Sansiques or Sansiquez). Marie seems to have both sold papers and sewn; newspapers described her as a seamstress who was only standing in for her man this once while he collected his batch of evening papers, but since Sansiquet would have needed to make that pickup every day, this sounds to me like an invention to highlight the poignant fluke of her being the only person standing in Place de Rennes below the station when Engine 721 burst out and the debris it sent flying crushed her.

By the way, when reporters wrote that the crash happened at 4:00 p.m. sharp, as proved by the clocks having stopped at that moment when the power was cut, they meant 4:00 p.m. by the clocks *inside* the station—so 4:05 by the outside clock and in the world outside the bubble of the railways. It wasn't until 1911, after twenty years of double time intended to give late passengers a little leeway, that the French companies changed their policy, advancing in-station clocks by five minutes to show the correct time.

Several reports on the Montparnasse Derailment assured readers that the Company of the West had promised the bereaved family a pension for life, or at least jobs for the boys. But when it was found that Jules Sansiquet had not been formally married to Marie Haguillard—a common situation among the working class—these vague offers were reduced to a death benefit of just three hundred francs. He moved his legal wife of twenty years (Léonie Célina Vanbos) into the rue Guilleminot home, and she replaced Marie as his partner selling papers till he died at age forty-five in 1898.

There is no evidence of either Sansiquet or the Company supporting Marie's boys. They lost their uncle Joseph the following August and somehow wound up two hundred kilometres away in the Normandy village of Saint-Martin-du-Bec. Julien died there in the Croismare Orphanage at age seven on September 22, 1896, less than a year after his mother.

Gaston survived in Saint-Martin-du-Bec to become a carpenter like his uncle and grandfather; he married in 1907, and, at age twenty-nine, gave his life for France on the Marne alongside tens of thousands of his countrymen.

Oddly, Marie Haguillard's was not the only death at Montparnasse Station on October 22. A hundred thousand people thronged to view the wreckage, many buying train tickets just to access the damaged platform, and one of them, a man named Augé, reportedly dropped dead in all the excitement.

———

The four crewmen of the Express were not sacked or even suspended, and neither were any of their bosses. At the inquiry the following spring, the train driver (the mechanic or engineer), **Guillaume** Marie **Pellerin** (1860–1931), was charged with wounding and homicide by imprudence, as was the senior guard (the conductor), Albert **Léon Mariette** (spelled in some sources as Marquet; 1853–1896).

The verdict of the inquiry was inconclusive. Blame was variously cast on the Westinghouse air brake for either fully or partially failing; on Pellerin for speeding and for taking too long to sound an alarm; on Mariette for being slow to respond to Pellerin's steam whistle (possibly due to his nodding off) and not trying his own air brake; and on the Company for relying too heavily on air brakes, imposing long shifts on drivers and onerous paperwork on guards, and tacitly rewarding speeding.

Guillaume Pellerin was sentenced to two months in prison and fined fifty francs, but both sentence and fine were suspended. He told journalists he had heart palpitations in the wake of the crash, but despite that, the whole second half of the driver's life still lay ahead of him; he lived another thirty-five years. His son followed father and grandfather into the profession.

Albert Léon Mariette received a lesser sentence, a fine of twenty-five francs, also suspended. Yet the senior guard died three weeks after the verdict, on April 21, 1896, at age forty-two. I have trouble believing that this was just a coincidence. Perhaps his leg never healed right and slowly poisoned his blood. Or could his guilt over failing to stop the train in time have weakened his health? Or even prompted him to take his own life?

Of course, nobody born in France in the nineteenth century counted on getting the biblical three score and ten, and especially not a railwayman; for all the security and benefits won by the union, these jobs were hard on the health. Guillaume's stoker, **Victor** Henry **Garnier** (1849–1899), died three years after the crash, at age forty-nine. **Jean Le Goff** (1866–1909), whose prompt response to Guillaume's steam whistle seems to be what saved the rest of the train from plunging over the parapet, lasted fourteen more years, advancing to stoker before he died at the age of forty-three.

An addition to the crew, some dozen of the passengers in *The Paris Express* are real people recorded as having been on the train when it derailed at Montparnasse.

Longtime deputy for Orne **Albert** Silas Médéric Charles **Christophle** (1830–1904) had his family's private carriage attached at Briouze in an unscheduled halt that put the Express behind schedule. I have drawn on the facts of Christophle's political career but invented almost everything about his private life. All I know about his wife, **Anna** Hefty **Christophle** (1834–1896), is that she died the year after the crash, at age sixty-two; Albert lived nine more years.

Riding in First Class was another deputy for Orne (and almost certainly Christophle's houseguest that week), the ammunition manufacturer **Jules-Félix Gévelot** (1826–1904), his wife, Adrienne **Emma** Boulart **Gévelot** (1845–1927), and an unidentified female friend of hers. A chevalier of the Legion of Honour like his colleague Christophle, Gévelot was the only passenger to give a detailed statement to the press. Also like Christophle, he lived just nine more years after the crash, but his young widow, Emma Gévelot, assumed the presidency of the French Society of Munitions and ran it for twenty-three years before she died, leaving everything to her goddaughter.

Although not travelling with Gévelot or Christophle, a third deputy for Orne, Adrien Charles Felix Marie, **comte de Lévis-Mirepoix** (1846–1928), and **Mathilde** Josephine **Riotteau L'Heureux** (1844–?), sister of a deputy from Manche, were also on the Express. I find it hard to accept this as a coincidence, so I have guessed that they were travelling as a couple.

Gévelot's unnamed maid and manservant boarded with

their employers at Briouze but rode in Third. Other travellers in that class included a maid, **Augustine Baudin** (or possibly Bardin or Boudin; born c. 1865), in service near Montparnasse. A **Monsieur Dois** told a journalist from *Le Matin* that he'd had to kick the door open to liberate himself and his carriage-mates and that as soon as they saw the state of the train, they burst out laughing at their narrow escape.

Joining the real-people-who-were-really-there on my passenger list are real people who could have been there, given that they were living in or near Paris in October 1895—plausible guests I have invited onto my train to populate *The Paris Express*.

All I know about **Jeanne Sarazin-Levassor** (1878–1896) is that she died the year after the derailment, at age eighteen. Three months after his stepdaughter's funeral, **Émile** Constans **Levassor** (1843–1897) decided that speed was the best medicine for grief. On the Lyon–Avignon leg of a ten-day car rally, he swerved to avoid a dog and was badly injured; his death, at his drawing table seven months later, was attributed to the lingering effects of the accident. Jeanne's twice-widowed mother, **Louise** Cayrol **Sarazin-Levassor** (1847–1916), who has been called the Mother of the Motorcar, steered her husband's company for another nineteen years.

The audacious plan of the country's engineer in chief **Fulgence Bienvenüe** (1852–1936) to build Paris an underground rail system was adopted in April 1896, and the first line opened a remarkably quick four years later. Bienvenüe, who married at age fifty-seven, is known as the Father of the Métro.

Marcelle de Heredia, later **Lapicque** (1873–1960), published research on nerve impulses on her own and with her tutor and later husband, Louis Lapicque, for sixty-five years. Her work earned her the Legion of Honour that her Cuban father, Severiano de Heredia, had been denied. The inseparable Lapicques adopted a nephew, Charles Thouvenin Lapicque, who grew up to be a painter. During World War II, Louis set up a French Résistance group in their lab, and Charles and his wife, Aline, hid Jews. They were later recognized as Righteous Among the Nations by the World Holocaust Remembrance Center.

Henry Ossawa Tanner (1859–1937) had his *Daniel in the Lions' Den* (1895, lost and now known only through a later copy) accepted for the 1896 Salon; he won a medal there the following year for his *Resurrection of Lazarus*. He married a Swedish-American opera singer in 1899, and he painted by the light of northern France, dividing his time between Paris and a Normandy farm, for another forty-two years.

Gaumont and Company (founded in 1895) is the oldest extant film company in the world. **Alice Guy,** later **Blaché** (1873–1968), secretary to **Léon Ernest Gaumont** (1864–1946), wrote, directed, and produced some seven hundred films, kicking them off with *The Fairy of the Cabbages* in 1896. The work of this forgotten Mother of Cinema includes the first full-length epic set in antiquity and the first "making of" feature.

Age seven in my novel, **Maurice** Raymond Gaston (or perhaps Gustave) **Marland** (1888–1944) served and was wounded in World War I, then settled in Granville and became a beloved teacher and, later, the leader of the local Résistance. In 1940 he helped fifty Allied soldiers escape from France. In 1944, when Marland was fifty-six, the German military police shot him dead and left him in a ditch.

Edmund **John** Millington **Synge** (1871–1909) would spent part of each year in Paris from 1894 to 1902 but he got most of his inspiration from long stays in the west of Ireland, in particular the Aran Islands. He wrote all his masterpieces for the stage (including *The Playboy of the Western World*) in the seven years before he died of lymphoma at thirty-seven.

Annah (c. 1880–fl. 1895?) is the only name we have for the teenage model who appears in photos by Alphonse Mucha and a painting known as *Annah la Javanaise* by Paul Gauguin. We know that when Gauguin was out of town in 1894, she sold off all his furniture and decamped, disappearing from the historical record; I have invented the rest and imagined a stage name of Annah Lamor.

Kiouaup (c. 1872–fl. 1895), son of the governor of the Kampong Tralach district in Cambodia, was listed as a student at the École Coloniale in Paris from 1887.

Max Jacob (born Max Alexandre, 1876–1944) dropped out of the Colo in 1897 and became a writer and painter in the Montmartre and Montparnasse avant-garde scenes. Gay and Jewish, the unpredictable Jacob converted to Catholicism and retired to a monastery, which did not save him from being—like many of his family—deported and murdered in the Holocaust.

Elise **Blonska** (1835–1897), a Russian (probably) émigrée who went by her last name only, was private secretary to various literary men but also a sort of volunteer social worker. In 1897, Blonska was staffing a stall at a Paris charity bazaar in a warehouse transformed into a medieval street with paint and papier-mâché when a cinematograph projector went up in flames. Among the more than one hundred and twenty charred bodies, Blonska's was identified by her orthopaedic corset.

Finally, **Madeleine** (born Anne) **Pelletier** (1874–1939), whom I have nicknamed **Mado**. This fiery feminist moved in radical circles in her teens; there is no evidence that she ever made a bomb, but she was certainly angry enough to do so. In her twenties Madeleine Pelletier prepared for the baccalauréat in that squalid back room she shared with the mother she loathed. Later, she enrolled at the Collège de Science and studied psychiatry, and she ended up working as a doctor in Montparnasse. A trouser-wearer, she founded a suffragist journal and started smashing windows. At sixty-five, she was arrested for giving an abortion to a thirteen-year-old incest victim and was sent not to prison but to an asylum, where she died in a matter of months.

The other passengers, both named (**Hakim, Cécile Langlois**) and unnamed, are my invention.

Author's Note

The Montparnasse Derailment caused barely a hiccup in the busy life of the station. After four days, Engine 721 was towed away with the help of horses; it turned out to require only minor repairs and was soon put back into service. The station façade was promptly rebuilt and stood until 1966, when a new station rose about three hundred and fifty metres to the southwest. Today the department store C&A occupies the site of the crash, just north of the Tour Montparnasse.

All the English translations of French sources quoted in the text and epigraphs of *The Paris Express* are my own very free interpretations.

I wrote this novel during a year (2022–2023) I was lucky enough to spend in Montparnasse, every wall of which bears some thumbprint of the past. "Our flesh keeps our memories," Charles-Louis Philippe wrote in *Bubu de Montparnasse,* his 1901 tale of street life; "we travel through the present with all our baggage." I am so grateful to the institutions that preserve—and make available—centuries of "baggage" of collective memory. I drew on more than forty articles about the derailment in twenty-six publications on Gallica (gallica.bnf. fr), the free online library of the Bibliothèque de France. To find out more about individual lives, especially uncelebrated ones such as those of the train crew and Marie Haguillard,

I ransacked the wonderful hoard of French bureaucracy at Filae.com.

Thomas Amossé, an expert on occupational history, was kind enough to puzzle out a census entry for me, and San Ní Ríocáin and Steph Gallaway gently corrected me when I mistook an *S* for an *L*. No journey like this is completed without help, and to the strangers and friends in many lands who compensate for my limitations, thank you so much, yet again.